(Homework snacks.)

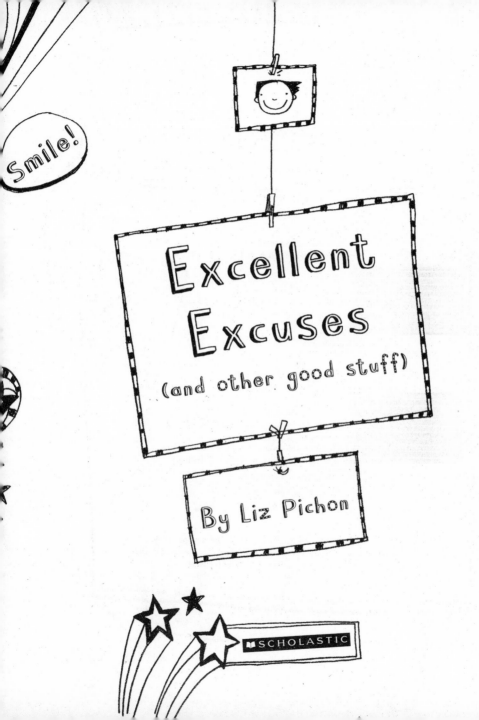

Smile!

Excellent Excuses

(and other good stuff)

By Liz Pichon

SCHOLASTIC

Scholastic Children's Books
An imprint of Scholastic Ltd

Copyright © Liz Pichon, 2011
The right of Liz Pichon to be identified as the author and
illustrator of this work has been asserted by her.

ISBN 978-93-5103-300-4

Tree
photograph
Pg: 21 courtesy
of
Lily Pichon
Flannery.

First edition: August 2014

This edition: September 2021

Printed in India at MicroPrints India, New Delhi

Wake up 👁 👁 this morning and
suddenly remember something absolutely

BRILLIANT!

I can forget ALL about lessons (and irritating things like Marcus Meldrew). And concentrate on GOOD stuff like:

☺ Inventing ✦new✦ ways to annoy my sister Delia. (So many!)

☺ Drawing pictures (that annoy Delia). Ha! Ha!

☺ Watching **TV** ⊙⊙ and eating caramel wafers.

☺ Eating caramel wafers and watching **TV**. ⊙⊙

And most importantly...

-Band practice for

 DOG ZOMBIES

with Derek
(who's my best mate and
next-door neighbour).

Tonight we're planning a sleepover
at his. Which is easy to do
as he's so close.

Excellent choice.

OK!

One of the other "great" things about going to Derek's is he doesn't have an annoying sister (like me) ...

... AND he has a dog called Rooster.

Woof

Which I know is a stupid name for a dog, but I'm getting used to it (sort of).

Sometimes Rooster can be 'almost' as annoying as Delia. Especially when he won't stop

BARKING!

Occasionally Derek throws him a Doggy Treat to shut him up.

Yum!

But if that doesn't work, I give him a pair of Delia's sunglasses to chew on. It keeps him happy for HOURS.

Right now I can hear Delia shuffling around outside my bedroom (which usually means trouble).

So I LEAN on my door to stop her from barging in.

Somehow she still manages to stick her BIG head around the door.

She says...

(That doesn't sound good ... groan.)

I wish I could shut Delia up with a doggy treat ... how good would that be?

When I see Mum, she's holding a letter from school. I'm trying really hard to remember

ANYTHING I've done

that might have got me into trouble.

NO ... can't think of anything. Nothing at all.

(I am innocent.)

But by the way **Mum** is looking at me, in that

What have you got to say for yourself?

kind of way, I must have forgotten something. She gives me the letter to read.

OK, just remembered.

To Mr and Mrs Gates
RE: Tom Gates Dog Attack

Dear Mr and Mrs Gates,

I do hope that Tom has recovered from the vicious dog that attacked him on the last day of term as he walked to school.

What luck that he had his schoolbook to defend himself with.

I'm SO glad it was only his homework that was chewed and not Tom. Enclosed is ANOTHER copy of the HOMEWORK – to review a film/book/TV show – for Tom to complete again during his holiday.

Let's hope there are no other **ANGRY** beasts ready to pounce in the future!

Many thanks for your help.

Kind regards

Mr Fullerman
Class 5F Form Tutor

I am trying to explain to Mum what happened to me by reenacting the whole scene in slow motion.

(There was no choice ... it was me or the homework.)

But she's not impressed. I think she suspects I might have made up the dog attack (I did).

Instead I have to agree to:

1. Do my review homework. (AGAIN.)

2. Not use vicious dogs as an excuse for lack of homework (or any other

Grrrr

10

kind of creature, for that matter).

3. **T**idy my room. (Mum added that one.)

Still, at
least I have

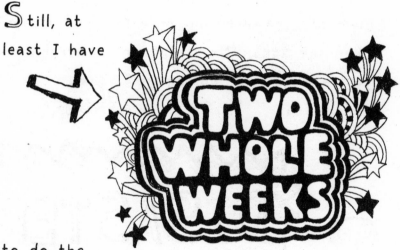

to do the
review homework in.
Though I will probably leave it until the last
possible moment, like the night before school.
That works for me.

"NOW?

What do you mean I have to do my homework right now? I've still got

TWO WHOLE WEEKS!"

Mum says, "There's no time like the present." Then she adds, "No sleepover at Derek's until you've done your homework."
Which is a

DISASTER!

I **have** to think of something to review quickly. Mmmmmmmmm. Think ... think ... think ... think ... think...

If I don't think of something **FAST** Mum will keep me in the house

FOR EVER.

Then just to add to the

PRESSURE,

Derek phones up to find out what time I'm coming over for the sleepover and band practice.

when

I hear Mum saying,

That all depends on how long it takes Tom to do his review homework, Derek.

(That's ALL I need.)

Mum thinks I should go to my room to ...

"sit quietly and concentrate" on getting it done".

(It's not working.)

So I do some drawing instead.

It's a lot more fun inventing my own
characters...

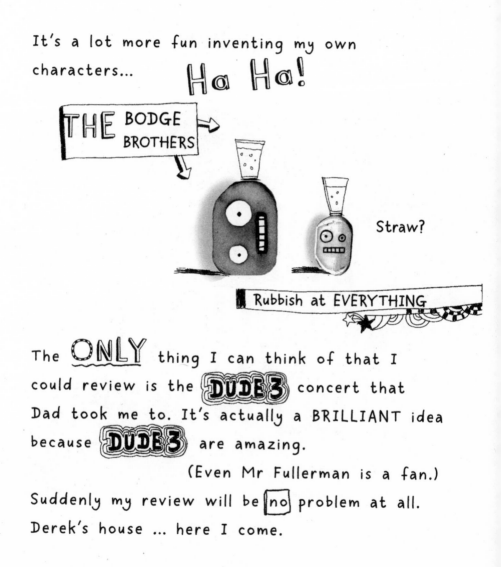

Ha Ha!

THE BODGE BROTHERS →

Straw?

Rubbish at EVERYTHING

The ONLY thing I can think of that I
could review is the DUDE3 concert that
Dad took me to. It's actually a BRILLIANT idea
because DUDE3 are amazing.

(Even Mr Fullerman is a fan.)

Suddenly my review will be no problem at all.
Derek's house ... here I come.

REVIEW HOMEWORK

By Tom Gates.

I went to see the DUDE3 concert.

They are the

BEST BAND IN THE WHOLE WIDE WORLD

and anyone who doesn't think so is a total IDIOT.

The End

I run downstairs and show it quickly to Mum.

There ... all done.

I am busy packing a few essentials
for Derek's house when
this time Dad comes up
to see me.
Apparently Mum
doesn't think I am taking my "review" homework
"seriously". Dad says I have do it again
"PROPERLY".

Which is a bit HARSH. (OK, I admit my
review was short, but true.)

Dad suddenly holds up a packet of
wafers.

"For the sleepover,
when you've done your
homework again, OK?"

WAFERS

SUDDENLY I am VERY INSPIRED.

In fact I have a TOTAL BRAIN WAVE
to get my homework done in double-quick time
(I am a genius). ☺

I *run d*
o
w
n stairs and grab
the first book from the shelf that
looks thick (but not <u>TOO</u> thick). Mum
sees that I am holding a BOOK and
assumes that:

TOM + THICK BOOK = SERIOUS ATTEMPT AT HOMEWORK.

(She looks pleased with me.) SIGH...

The book I've got is about ...
let me see ... ⊙ ⊙

TREES!

Never mind, that will have to do. I can see
there's a lot of good stuff written on
the back of this book (and inside!) that
will help make my REVIEW seem very
impressive indeed.

Here goes.

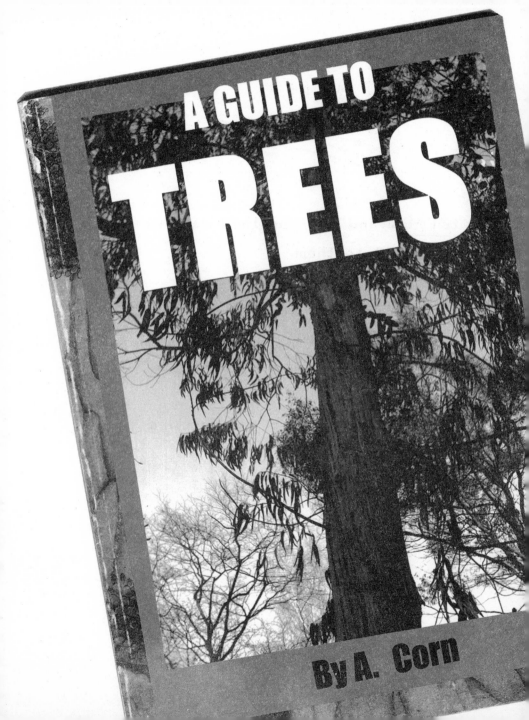

A GUIDE TO
TREES

By A. Corn

Homework FINISHED.

YEAH!

I tell Mum and Dad and they want me to
READ it to them.

"What, NOW?" 😟

"Yes, Tom, now. We'd love to hear it."

(Which actually means - just checking you've
really done it this time.)

SLAM

Delia is lurking in the kitchen trying to listen. So I shut the kitchen door (in her face), then read it as ⊱⊰━━━━━ quickly as I can.

LUCKILY, my homework is EXCELLENT (if I do say so myself).

Mum and Dad are pleased 😊 and slightly surprised I've managed to write **such** a good review SO quickly. I let them see it by *WAFTING* it under their noses ... super fast.

WAFT

(Must remember to hide the book on trees too.)

Mum and Dad say well done for being

so FOCUSED.

I say, "It's all down to

GOOD PARENTING."

(Which is something I've heard my teachers say.)
Then I add, "I'm actually VERY interested
in TREES." (I'm not.)

SO SWEET

This goes down really well and
stops Mum and Dad from asking me any more
difficult questions.

GREAT!

(I should say nice stuff like that more often.)

They are both in a good mood 😊 now so I suggest that another sign of

GOOD PARENTING

would be to reward my hard work and EFFORT with some

EXTRA

pocket money?

Which doesn't go down quite so well...

No chance.

(Worth a try, though.)

SLEEPOVER
AT DEREK'S.

Yeah!

Derek is happy

I've brought ➡️ SNACKS.

But stupidly, 😞 I've forgotten to bring my

guitar for band practice. **A**nd far more importantly, I've left

my special teddy at home. (I don't tell Derek because we agreed that Special Teddies were probably a bit **TOO** babyish now we're in a band.)

 ← WRONG

Luckily Derek's house is only next door to mine. So I nip back home to get them both.

Delia is sitting in the front garden with her "dodgy" boyfriend Ed (or Ted or whatever his name is). He says, All right, Tom? (Which is nice and takes me by surprise.) Then Delia shouts,

Get lost ... idiot.

(Which is not a surprise at all.)

That's when I notice Ed and Delia are actually UGH! HOLDING hands.

It's HORRIBLE.

I feel a bit sick and have to run into the house quickly.

I grab my guitar, teddy AND a selection of embarrassing photos of Delia that I've been saving for a VERY special occasion.

I think this might be the SPECIAL occasion I've been waiting for.

Delia with a potty on her head.

Delia after cutting her own hair with play scissors.

Delia after I pushed her into the mud (my personal favourite).

Delia with scary smile.

Delia with more bad hair and spots.

Derek can't stop laughing at Delia's OLD photos.

Ha! Ha! Ha! Ha! Ha! Ha!

We both agree that photos this funny need to be shared with OTHER people.

Other people like

Delia's boyfriend ED.

(I have a good plan.)

We cleverly attach all the photos (plus a few extra drawings) to Derek's fishing line. Then we dangle them out of the ⊞⊞ just behind Delia's head.

huh?

Our plan seems to be working. **E**d is **laughing** a lot. Unlike Delia, who is wondering *what* he's laughing at.

Luckily we manage to pull up the photos before Delia works out what's going on. At least they're not holding hands any more.

SUCCESS!

(It's a good start to the sleepover.)

DOG ZOMBIES

Band Practice

next. **M**r Fingle

(Derek's dad)

is hovering outside the garage where we practise. Derek says we can't start until his dad is **OUT** of the way completely.

This is because he likes to give us **tips** on music, which Derek finds **very** embarrassing. Mind you, my dad is **EXACTLY** the same. (What is it with dads and music? ♪ ♪ ♪). **M**r Fingle keeps his record collection and record player in the garage.

All his records are in alphabetical order and Derek says he spends HOURS cleaning them and looking at the covers. (How sad is that?)

Anytime we go to practise, Mr Fingle will suddenly appear and say things like,

That's not music, ♪ THIS is music!

or

In MY day, music sounded like REAL music ... blah blah blah.

Derek warns me...

"If my dad EVER says to you,

'Have you heard of this band, Tom?'

just say YES.

What happens if I say NO? I ask.

"You'll be forced to listen to CRACKLY OLD records FOR EVER. So trust me. Just say YES and pretend you know all about the band already."

OK, I agree.

He's still there.

We wait until Mr Fingle is safely out of the way before sneaking in and getting started.

If we are **EVER** going to become like **DUDE 3** (*BEST* band in the world)

we need to learn a few more songs. Which won't be easy because right now the ONLY song we can play all the way through (just about) is **DELIA'S A WEIRDO**

Which goes like this...

Delia's a Weirdo

Who's that weirdo over there?
Dressed in **black**
With greasy hair
You can't trust her
She's not nice
She's got no heart
Just a block of ice

CHORUS   Delia
She's a WEIRDO
Delia
She's a GEEK
Delia
She's a WEIRDO
Delia
She's a FREAK

Delia's a grumpy moo
Don't let her
Stand next to you
Big black glasses
Hide her eyes
She really smells
And that's no lie

CHORUS

Delia enjoying
the song.

Derek plays me a song called

WILD THING

(It's an oldie his dad taught him.)

It's ACE! But I think we might need

another band member to play it properly.

I don't think Derek can keep playing drums and

keyboard ...

... at the same time.

Luckily, Derek agrees.

TRIP

We are chatting about how to find a new band member when his dad suddenly appears.

TV advert

MASSIVE POSTER ✓

NEW BAND MEMBER?
I'm available!

Derek says, "We're busy, Dad," but Mr Fingle doesn't take the hint.

"What are you playing, lads?"

"WILD THING" ... Mr Fingle,

I say. Derek gives me a "what did you say THAT for?" look.

"'Wild Thing'. Good choice, boys. Didn't I teach you that, Derek?"

Derek's not listening. He is trying to get his dad to leave. It's not working.

NOT NOW DAD

"Do you know who played the original version of 'Wild Thing'?" Mr Fingle asks.

(In my head I'm thinking about what Derek told me.)

So I say... "YES."

Then Mr Fingle says,

"Really? Did you know the The Wild Ones recorded it in 1965, but it's **The Troggs'** version that everyone remembers."

Now it gets tricky.

M r Fingle then asks me,

"Have you heard of **The Troggs**, Tom?"

And for a split second I forget what I'm
supposed to say (because I've said YES
already, and I don't want to be rude). I hear
myself saying,

NO, Mr Fingle, I haven't heard of The Troggs.

And that's it ... he's Off!

Looking through his record collection to play us
the original version of Wild Thing.
Derek rolls his eyes and says
we might as well leave him
to it.

Oh no...

"He won't even notice we're gone," Derek says.

He's right.

Derek and I spend the rest of the evening chit-chatting about Delia's dodgy photos (VERY funny).

And how **BRILLIANT** it was

sneaking back to my house and

sticking even MORE photos around

when Delia wasn't looking!

Delia's photos + me and Derek = Genius

Mrs Worthington's moustache gets a

mention too.

* ☾ *

It's getting late and I'm really tired, but I don't want to be the first one to go to sleep because I'm waiting for the right moment to bring out my teddy.

Then Derek says that
"JUST FOR TONIGHT" he's going to use
his ➡️ 🐼 teddy as a PILLOW

because it helps him sleep. 🐻😴

And I say, "That's SUCH a good idea!" And
take my teddy 🧸 out too.

Then we eat some snacks ...
and a few more. Until we both fall
fast asleep zzzzzzzzzzzzzzzzzzzzzzzzzzzzzzzzzzzzzzzzzzzzzzzzzzzzzzzzzzzzzzzzzzzzzzzz

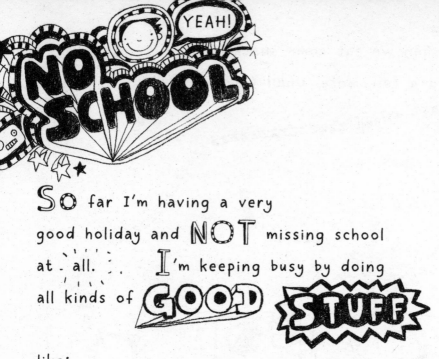

YEAH!

NO SCHOOL

SO far I'm having a very good holiday and NOT missing school at all. I'm keeping busy by doing all kinds of GOOD STUFF

like:

☺ Finding NEW places to hide

Delia's sunglasses.

☺ Sleepovers at Derek's.

☺ Listening to **DUDE 3** and trying out new **ROCK STAR** poses.

☺ More drawing and doodling.

This is a good game...

Do a scribble

then see what you can turn it into.

Like ⬆ this ... ALIENS!

This game is particularly good to play in BORING ⊖ ⊖ lessons, as it looks like you are VERY busy.

 ← (mmm? any ideas?)

I am perfectly happy and have 😊
LOADS of ideas for more drawings when
Dad comes in and interrupts.

Are you ready?

 "What for?"

"Remember? You're staying at your cousins'
for the afternoon."

"What for?"

"Because your mum and I are both working.
It's just for a few hours."

"Can I go to Derek's?"

"The Fingles are out
shopping today."

groan

"The ?"

"You mean Granny and Granddad?
They're out and about too."

"I'll stay here with Delia."

"You must be desperate, Tom. She's going out.
Sorry, you have to go to your cousins'. Just
try not to do anything silly ... like last time."

(The Fossils... "out and about.")

GROAN ... looks like I don't have much choice. Then Dad adds,

"Oh, and **PLEASE** DO **NOT** mention my

birthday to Uncle Kevin or

Aunty Alice. I don't want

any fuss this year."

Surprise!

Dad's birthday last year

"OK."

"And don't mention how many parking tickets I have ... Uncle Kevin doesn't need to know."

"OK."

There seem to be a LOT of things I'm not allowed to mention to Uncle Kevin and Aunty Alice. I sometimes don't remember them all.

parking tickets, birthdays

Last time I was there for a visit, Uncle Kevin kept asking Dad about his job. And I heard Dad say...

"Well, I've just moved to a fantastic NEW office that is much closer to home . So I do a lot less travelling and it's far more suitable for my work." So I said...

Dad's office is in the *GARDEN*

... it's a shed. ➡ ⬅

Which is TRUE!

But Dad gave me one of those

"what did you have to say

that for?" stares.

I definitely don't mention the tin

of biscuits 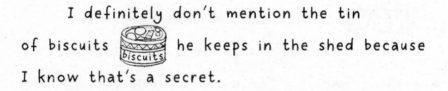 he keeps in the shed because

I know that's a secret.

Occasionally my cousins

play tricks on me. He He He He

Some tricks are funnier than others.
This one was annoying.

It was REALLY embarrassing when
Aunty Alice followed
the chocolate
footprints right back to me.

(One reason I don't want to go to the
cousins'.)

So I am (very slowly) getting ready to go, when Delia comes up to me and says...

"If you're going to the cousins', will you do me a favour?"

"What?"

"DON'T COME BACK ... EVER."

SUDDENLY I think of some

GOOD reasons to go after all.)

1. Delia won't be there to annoy me. ☺

2. They keep LOTS of cakes and biscuits in the house.

3. There's **MASSIVE**

TVs all over the house.

4. And EXTRA **LARGE**

SOFT
←COMFY→
SOFAS

How bad can it be? ☺

On the drive over, Dad is trying to remember if he has money for the parking meter. I can tell he's a bit grumpy today.

He says,

"Don't get chocolate stuck under your shoes again..."

(That was the cousins' fault!)

"AND don't break anything that's expensive."

"Everything in their house is expensive, Uncle Kevin said so."

This cushion is very expensive.

"Did he? Well just because something is EXPENSIVE, Tom," Dad says as we drive up to Uncle Kevin's BIG house, "doesn't mean it's better, or any more ... well, TASTEFUL."

Dad is very pleased Uncle Kevin has already gone. "I can park in his space for free," he says.

Aunty Alice opens the door and tells us,

"You've just missed your Uncle Kevin!" Come in!

And Dad says,
"What a SHAME! We did try to get here earlier."

(We didn't.)

Then Dad thanks Aunty Alice for having me and promises not to be too long. BYE!

I go and find the cousins, who are busy eating snacks

 (which is a good start).

But they don't seem keen on
sharing their snacks with me.

      Instead we go to the food
cupboard (which is STUFFED full of
treats). The cousins tell me to help myself.

    "You're a guest, take those biscuits ...
they're nice."

BRILLIANT!

(It would be rude not to.)

I manage to ➡ CRAM ⬅ LOTS

into my pockets and carry the rest in

a BIG pile.

Which is so high I can't see ⊙ ⊙ where

I'm going. The cousins help out by shouting

directions.

"Forward."

"Forward."

"Keep going...

Keep going." "KEEP GOING ...
WHOOPS!"

I walk

BANG

SMACK into Aunty Alice.

 Who suggests I
put a few snacks back.
(I think the cousins have
tricked me.) I'm allowed to keep the caramel
wafers and a drink. Which is good news
because at least I get to do the "empty biscuit
wrapper" joke on the cousins...

Which they fall for

EVERY TIME.

(It's hilarious.)

When the cousins have had enough of my little biscuit joke, I suggest we watch TV instead.

"GOOD IDEA," they say.

"Let's watch something FUNNY?"
I add. But the cousins want to watch a

SCARY film. (Which is not my idea

of fun at ALL.)
I blame ➡ 👩 Delia. She let me

watch 👀

THE HOUSE WITH THE DEADLY EYES

when I was little. She thought it was funny
making me JUMP
(it wasn't).

Ha ha

But I don't tell the cousins that I REALLY don't like SCARY films.

Instead I say...

"I'll watch ANYTHING."

They choose...

VAMPIRE SWAMP MONSTERS FROM HELL

(Mmm, doesn't look too bad?)

OK, I'm wrong.

The film turns out to be <u>the</u> most

film I have EVER seen. ⊙ ⊙ I have to hide

behind a cushion for most of it. Unlike the

cousins, who can't stop LAUGHING! They

think it's funny (it's not).

I can't wait until it's over.

Aunty Alice pops in. She says,

You all seem to be enjoying yourselves!

"Loads," I say.

When it's finished, the cousins suggest we watch **ANOTHER** film. (Groan.)

"A REALLY SCARY film this time."
(What do they mean, a REALLY SCARY one?)

Great, I'll just have to keep my eyes SHUT →← the ENTIRE time now.

They put on:

So I am hiding behind a cushion again.

It's not helping much.

I can still hear the scary stuff

through the cushion.

Luckily Dad turns up early to pick me up.

PHEW!

I AM SAVED.   Hooray

HOORAY!

In front of the cousins, though, I pretend to

be VERY sad that I won't get to see the

rest of the film. SHAME.

"Maybe next time you're round," the cousins

say to me. (I hope not.)

Aunty Alice tells Dad I've been "no trouble at all".

For some reason Dad asks, "No chocolate stains on the carpet or antiques broken, then?"

(Thanks for reminding everyone, Dad.)

"Nothing damaged. But speaking of old antiques ... isn't it your birthday soon, Frank?"

And I hear Dad say, "My birthday's not for AGES ". Which isn't true at ALL. So I mention that Dad's birthday is actually NEXT WEEK. How could anyone forget their own birthday?

Aunty Alice INSISTS that we should all go out and celebrate.

"Just like last year. It will be

(Dad's birthday present last year.)

Dad doesn't seem keen on the idea. I can tell he's trying very hard to think of reasons not to go when Uncle Kevin bursts in through the door.

"Frank! I hope you paid for parking. There's a traffic warden looking at your car."

From the way Dad *RUNS* out of the door, I'm guessing he didn't buy a ticket.

We all follow him outside.

Dad is **REALLY CROSS** and shouting rude things. Uncle Kevin is shaking his head in a disapproving way.

So I tell Uncle Kevin that HE'D be "CROSS" too if he had TEN

parking tickets like Dad.

Now Dad's cross with ME for saying how many tickets he's got.

Like it's MY FAULT!

Dad's in a REALLY bad mood all the way home. But that's NOTHING compared with how cross MUM is when she finds out that:

You've done What?

1. **D**ad got **ANOTHER** parking ticket (number eleven).

2. **W**e <u>have</u> to go to dinner with the cousins for Dad's birthday.

3. **I** watched Vampire Swamp Monsters From Hell (well, sort of).

I don't think I'll be going back to the cousins' again for a while, which means I won't be able to watch the rest of

BLOODSUCKER BEETLES vs GIANT ALIENS.

(RESULT!)

During the night I wake up (·) (·) with a HORRIBLE PAIN

in my Agh! tooth. I sneak to the bathroom to take a proper look.

HOLE

It's not good. I can see a **BIG** black hole in it ...

oh no

... groan.

I brush my teeth in the hope ☺ that the hole will suddenly close up and go away.

It doesn't. It just **HURTS** even more.

Which means I'll probably HAVE to go to the DENTIST now.

GROAN.

If Mum finds out I have a toothache she won't let me have ANY sweets or snacks for a while. And she DEFINITELY won't let me take treats over to DEREK'S house.

My treats

Mum's treats

TOO late.

Mum must have heard me in the

bathroom groaning and has woken up.

I'm poking my tooth when she knocks on the

door. I tell Mum that I can't sleep

because I have a headache. And

I'm having "bad dreams"

from watching the SCARY film at the

cousins'.

Poor TOM Mum gives me some medicine

(which brilliantly stops my tooth

hurting).

I go back to bed and try to get

some sleep.

zzzzzzzzz

82

But in the morning my toothache

is **BACK**. 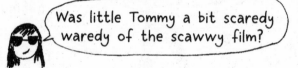 And if that's not bad enough ...

... the first thing **DELIA** says to me is,

 Was little Tommy a bit scaredy waredy of the scawwy film?

GREAT ... Mum must have told her I woke up in the night. On top of calling me a scaredy cat, she keeps on sneaking up behind me and saying

 BOO!

which is getting on my nerves.

So I do this drawing to cheer me up.

I'm eating breakfast on the non-painful side of my mouth (and trying not to dribble) when Derek comes round and asks if I want to go swimming.

(Which might take my mind off this toothache.)

So I say yes and hope for the best. At least Delia won't be there to annoy me.

Question: What's more irritating – Delia or toothache?

Answer: Delia – because eventually toothache goes away.

MY SWIMMING Shame

I've been *groaning*

a bit due to my tooth

⇨ **A THROBBING**,,, Derek asks me

if I'm OK. I don't mention my toothache because I'm hoping the water will SOOTHE my face and make it go away completely.

AND Derek has TREATS for after swimming that he said he'd share with me. Instead I tell him that my groaning is due to Delia SHOVING me and injuring my arm. Which is true ... she did.

Derek is very glad ☺ he doesn't have a sister like me.

I'm happy with a dog.

When we get to the pool, it's pretty busy already. I spot quite a few kids from our school swimming, including ...

Amy is the smartest girl in the school, which is excellent for me as I get to take the occasional sneaky peak 👁 👁 at her work.

The girls are too busy chatting and swimming and don't see us come in.

Derek and I decide to play it cool and only say hello to them if they say hello to us first.

(Good plan.)

So we go off to get changed and I'm

Rummaging around in my bag

looking for my blue swimming trunks.

I can't find them ANYWHERE.

I have a HORRIBLE feeling I've left them at home. (I have.)

Derek makes two suggestions:

1. I should swim in my PANTS. (That's <u>not</u> going to happen.)

2. He has a very OLD pair of trunks in his bag I can borrow.

I say, "GREAT." At least I'll be able to swim now.

Derek passes them to me under the changing room door.

When I see them, I'm wondering exactly how old these trunks really are? The teddy bear pattern makes me think Derek was probably about FOUR when he last wore them.

They are a bit short so I have to keep my towel round me until the very LAST minute. Then I quickly jump in the pool and hope no one has seen me.

Derek and I swim
up and down and do
some diving, which is fun. ☺

(It makes me forget about my toothache
... well, almost.)

Amy and her friends still haven't seen us
yet, but **Norman Watson** has. ⊙ ⊙

He's waving like **CRAZY**
from the other
side of the pool. Norman's
brought his little brother with
him, who looks just like him only
smaller. They come and join us, which is good
because [now] we can all play **SHARK**
together.

$\mathbb{D}$erek is the SHARK first.

He manages to swim and catch me. Now it's

my turn to be the SHARK. YEAH! I spot

Norman (who's not great at hiding) and quickly

swim to catch him. Now Norman is the

SHARK. I've never seen Norman swim

before... So it's a bit of a surprise when he

starts to SPLASH!

He's not moving much, just ...

His arms and legs are thrashing around

making **MASSIVE**

waves in the pool. The splash is SO huge the lifeguard looks over and blows her whistle. We're all told to:

GET OUT OF THE WATER!

The lifeguard dives in and "rescues" Norman (who's **not** drowning, just swimming VERY badly).

Everybody is standing at the side of the pool watching (including Amy, Florence and Indrani).

While Norman is explaining to the lifeguard about his "unusual swimming style", the lifeguard tells us,

"No more crazy splashing or you'll have to get OUT!"

It's VERY embarrassing.

Then if **THAT'S** not bad enough, Amy comes over and says to me,

"Nice teddy swimming trunks, Tom."

(I'd forgotten all about my teddy-bear swimming trunks ... groan.)

And I can hear Florence and Indrani laughing.

I jump back in the pool quickly to hide.

Norman's little brother Alfie jumps in too and wants to challenge me to a race.

He's only small, I don't want to hurt his feelings ...

so I give him a head start.

RACE YOU!

How was I supposed to know Alfie's swimming "style" was even

WORSE than Norman's?

(The lifeguard has seen enough splashing for one day.)

It was a short swim, but on the way home I realize that my toothache 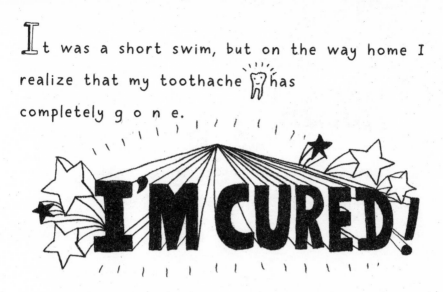 has completely g o n e.

I'M CURED!

I won't have to go to the dentist after all now.

BRILLIANT!

WATER + SPLASHING = TOOTHACHE CURE

I celebrate by taking the very small sweet that Derek offers me.

AGHHHH!

(Which is a mistake.)

LAST DAY OF HOLIDAY

Bad news is ... my tooth is still throbbing quite badly. I can't believe the holiday has gone **SO** **FAST** and I'm back at school tomorrow.

If I tell Mum about my tooth, I could probably get the day off school. But that would mean having to:

1. Go to the DENTIST.

2. **G**et stuff done to my tooth.

3. **N**ot eat **TREATS** or any

sweet stuff for a very long time.

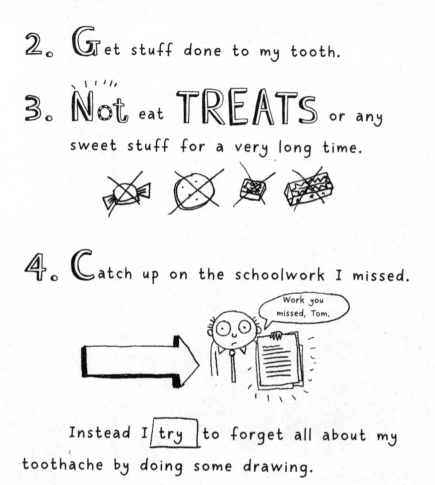

4. **C**atch up on the schoolwork I missed.

Work you missed, Tom.

Instead I try to forget all about my

toothache by doing some drawing.

My drawings

...I'm STILL thinking

about my
TOOTHACHE.

(Groan.)

I know, I'll do a BIG poster for
DOGZOMBIES instead.

Derek and I definitely want a drummer
for the band. We can put the poster on the
school noticeboard tomorrow.
It will GRAB everyone's attention.

(That's the plan, anyway.)

That should do the trick.

(Tooth still hurting, though.)

BACK TO SCHOOL

I'm struggling to get out of bed even more than usual. (I didn't sleep so well; $\ominus$ $\ominus$ tooth still throbbing.) School starts in half an hour and I have a LOT of things to remember today, like...

☺ LUNCH

☺ MY REVIEW HOMEWORK

important → ☺ DOGZOMBIES DRUMMER POSTER ☆

☺ PE KIT

(Or I'll be forced to wear something from the SPARE KIT BOX.)

SPARE KIT BOX

I eat breakfast carefully (on the good side of my mouth.) Mum tells me to get a move on!

She thinks I'm suffering from "BacktoSchoolitis".

"Very common on the first day back at school."

Delia says, "He's got

Irritating Brother Syndrome."

(Which is annoying.)

Dad asks me, "Have you got your lunch? Got your homework?"

"Got worms?" Delia adds.

Normally I would defend myself with

a HILARIOUS and funny

answer. But I think the toothache has stopped

that part of my brain from

working properly

Funny part
of the
brain

... for now.

Derek and I are a bit late for school.

We try and do fast walking while I show

Derek the

He's impressed and offers to put the

poster up for me.

"You'll forget," he says.

(Harsh but true.)

Back in class, it's like we've never been away. Marcus Meldrew manages to ANNOY me within TWO seconds of sitting down at my desk.

He pulls up his school jumper and shows me his T-shirt.

I can't believe it!

He's wearing a special DUDE3 T-shirt that the WHOLE band have signed!

"It's NEW and the signatures are hand-stitched on so they won't ever wash out."

"I'm ffwwilled for you, Marcus," I say.

(My tooth is throbbing, so I'm finding it hard to speak properly.)

Mr Fullerman begins to call the register and I answer,

"Earrrrr, suuurrrrr."

He thinks I'm trying to be funny.
 Ha! Ha! (I'm not!)
Then the class start laughing and Mr Fullerman peers over the register.
His beady eyes are fixed on ME.

He says,

"TOM ... I hope you've remembered your REVIEW HOMEWORK. You've had two weeks to do it. And a letter to remind you."

And I say, "Eeeerrrrrrrrrrr" (to give myself time to think).

Because I CAN'T believe I've gone and forgotten it!

What I SHOULD have said to Mr Fullerman is:

"Sorry, sir. I <u>have</u> done it, but I forgot it. I'll bring it in tomorrow."

I apologize...

But for some STUPID reason I hear myself saying:

"Sir, it's like this...
My dad got a really BAD

LURGY bug over the holidays, then we ALL got it. The doctor said it was <u>VERY</u> catching and the bugs could be \\\\\,,,,,,,,,,,,,,,

EVERYWHERE,

including the paper I wrote my homework on.

So I just have to write it out again on
LURGY -FREE paper
just to be on the safe side.

I'll bring it in tomorrow ...
promise."

(Why, why? Why did I say that?)
Mr Fullerman says,

"Tom, is there something wrong with your mouth?"

Because [this] is what I *actually* said:

"Errr, it's wike thisss...

My daaa go a wearrrly add

WURGY bug ower the howidays, hen we AWW go it. The doctow said it was verwy caaching and thw uggs coowld bee EVERRWYWHERE, incwuding th aper I wwott eye omeworwk on.

Seww I ust ave too wwitte it owwt again on WURRGY-FWWEE apper usst to ee on the affe ide. I'ww bwing it in ommorow ... pwomise."

I managed to mutter,

   "Sore twooth, sirr ... I'm OK wrreally."

Mr Fullerman looks at me suspiciously. He carries on with the register but thinks I'm up to something.

   (Like I'm doing this deliberately!)

Amy and Marcus have both moved away from me because I said the word **LURGY** too many times.

"I have twoothache ... not the LURGY," I tell **A**my.

(She might feel sorry for me.)

But she's ignoring me and staring at the classroom door.

"Tom, isn't that your dad waving at you?"

MY DAD?

I look up and see someone who looks a bit like my dad?

IT IS MY DAD.

He's trying to get my attention by waving my homework around (it looks like he's swatting flies). Groan.

Now EVERYONE is STARING at him, including Mr Fullerman, who goes over to the door. He looks a bit CROSS at being disturbed.

Dad starts talking to him ... ha! ha! and they BOTH start LAUGHING.

ha! ha!

What's SO funny?

(This is going to be embarrassing, I can feel it.)

Mr Fullerman takes my work and Dad makes
a thumbs-up sign at me

(with the rest of the class still watching).

Then Mr Fullerman comes in and says in
front of EVERYONE:

**"Tom, your dad has very kindly
dropped in your review homework.
He also assures me that he's totally
LURGY free and so is your homework.
Which must be a HUGE relief to the
WHOLE CLASS, I'm sure."**

(The shame...)

At least Mr Fullerman has my homework now ...
I suppose.

I hope today gets better.
(Though it's not looking promising.)

It's no good.

My tooth is hurting SO much.

I can't concentrate any more

groan.

Mr Fullerman sees that my face has

SWELLED UP

a LOT. He sends me

straight to the sick

room...

Not good

On the way to the sick room, I walk past some little kids who stare at me like I'm some kind of MONSTER.

E ven M rs Mumble *Oh dear, Tom.* in the school office looks concerned. She rings my *What's Tom done NOW?* dad straight away. He's only just got home when he has to come straight back to school.

M y tooth hurts SO badly I don't even care that he is wearing a STUPID T-shirt. *Shame...* Dad makes me an emergency appointment at the dentist and we drive straight there.

MY DENTIST

Most dentists try and make you feel

chilled and relaxed by having things

like fish tanks and soothing music

(to drown out the sound of

DRILLING).

But my dentist is a bit different.

He has a SCARY-looking metal crocodile

with sharp teeth on the wall. As well as

posters of people with rotten

teeth and gum diseases.

(I think he's trying to make a point.)

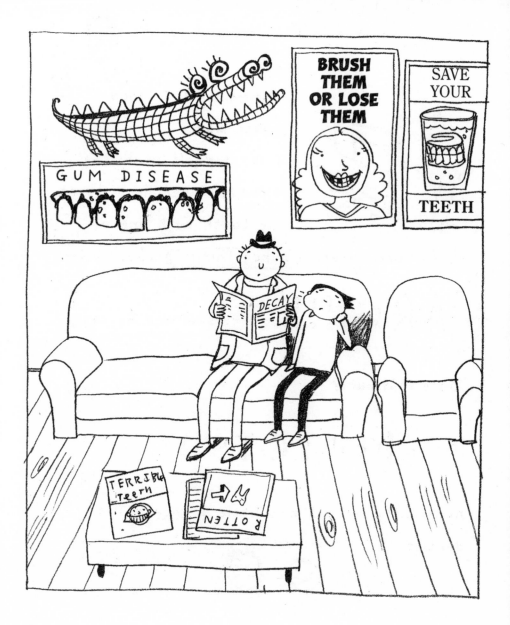

Mr Kay takes a look at me and says,

"Mmmmm, not good, young man."

(Like I don't know that already.) Then he picks at my tooth with one of those horrid metal pokey things.

"ARGH!!" I scream and he says,

"Does that hurt?"

(Errrrr, YES! LOTS!)

Apparently when I was little I once BIT a dentist.

ow Mum thinks that they have a

warning on my file like this:

WARNING
TOM GATES

NAME: TOM GATES

BEWARE

THIS BOY BITES

TAKE **EXTREME** CARE
WHEN APPROACHING THIS CHILD
AS HE CAN BE DANGEROUS AND
UNPREDICTABLE.

CAUTION NEEDED!

Mr Kay explains EVERYTHING to me before he does it. (In case I turn vicious.)

 He says,

"Raise your hand if you feel any pain at all."

So I raise my hand ... even though he hasn't started yet.

Groan ... now he has.

I get through the injections, drilling and filling by keeping my eyes tightly ⟶ ⟵ shut and thinking of different ways of getting my own back on Delia for teasing me.

When I do open them, I can see a WEIRD mobile hanging from the ceiling.

I think it's made of teeth?

It is made of teeth.

Mr Kay points at it and says,
"That's what happens when you **don't** look after
your teeth."

It's really freaky.

I'm SO relieved when it's all over. ☺

My face is numb and I end up dribbling
the pink [ ] water Mr Kay
gives me to swish round my mouth everywhere.

Dad says I am VERY brave.

I agree ☺ and suggest maybe

a small treat might be in order?

Mr Kay suddenly remembers to give me some
"special stickers".

(They're not exactly my idea of a treat, but
I'm guessing something SWEET will be out
of the question now?)

Interesting selection of stickers

We stop off to pick up the tablets I have to take (I don't want my face to SWELL up again).

Dad likes my stickers. He thinks it's

HILARIOUS that my dentist is called **Mr D. Kay**...

"A dentist called Mr D. KAY - that's IRONIC," he says.
I have no idea what he's talking about.

Dad buys me a comic for a treat instead. When we get home, Mum is being
very nice to me too. Unlike Delia,   Ha!

Ha!

who thinks it's funny to
offer me SWEETS.

Then she takes them away,
saying, "Oh, sorry, I forgot
you've just been to the
dentist. Ha! Ha!"

Mum catches Delia tormenting me and tells
her off. (Yes, Delia, back off.)

Then Mum says that I can eat my (non-chewy)
dinner on a tray in front of the telly without
Delia bothering me.

It's bliss.

After dinner Dad reminds me to take my tablet. I'm looking at the bottle and FINALLY I get Dad's dentist name joke...

Mr D. Kay.

Mr Decay.

Hilarious!

BACK
At School

This morning Mum says I am well enough to go to school today despite me doing a "sad face". (It was worth a try.)

At least she gives me a REAL sick note that says:

Dear Mr Fullerman,

Please could Tom be excused from PE just for now as he has a nasty tooth infection which has almost cleared up.

Kind regards,

Rita Gates

But I might try and change it to ... ALL WEEK or <u>ALL MONTH</u>.

(Give it a go?)

At school, I'm busy telling a group of friends about my **DEADLY** and **DANGEROUS** tooth experience.

"It took my dentist ~~one~~ ~~two~~ ~~three~~ SEVEN WHOLE hours to save it AND the dental nurse almost *FAINTED*."

Everyone looks impressed.

So I add, "The dentist said I was very very brave."

(That bit's true.)

Norman tells us about the time he got his head ⟹ trapped ⟸ in some railings and had to be rescued by firemen. (Why am I not surprised?)

My mate SOLID shows us the scar on his arm from when he fell off his bike.

It looks like a long zip.

Derek once got stuck in a cat flap (he's NEVER told me that before!).

Then Mark Clump rolls up his trousers and shows us something that looks like two dots on his leg.

"What's that?" I ask.

"Snake bite," he says. We all take a closer look.

WOW! hmmm   Marcus Meldrew pretends he's not very impressed at all.

He says,

"Huh! That's nothing. I was bitten by
my new pet."

"Really? Have you got a snake too, Marcus?"
Derek asks.

"My pet is FAR more scary than a snake."

"What is it ... a man-eating

SPIDER?" I say.

hungry

"**I**'ve got a VERY BIG new dog.

Fetch

I'm training him right now."
"A dog ... like how big a dog?"

"**HUGE** ... he's a bit **WILD**. I had to
fight him off and that's when he chewed me...
I've got a bad scar."

"Let's see the scar, then?" Norman asks.
"No, it's still VERY painful."
Marcus rubs his leg and walks away
with a slight limp.

FAKE
Limp

(I think Marcus is telling fibs.)

"Mind you," I say, "if I was a
dog, I'd bite Marcus too."
Derek agrees with me.

Then Mr Keen (the headmaster) blows the
whistle to go into school and
makes us JUMP.

 PEEP! His face gets redder with
every puff. It looks like a
BIG RED tomato now.
PEEP!

And that's when I suddenly remember

I have a VERY good reason to:

AVOID Mr Keen.

This is because last term Mr Keen heard me singing "Delia's a Weirdo", a song I wrote about Delia.*

He immediately put me in the school concert! Which could have been **total humiliation** in front of the whole school. (Mostly due to lack of practise and slightly rude lyrics about Delia.) Luckily Derek came to my rescue and saved me from possible singing shame.

(*See p. 191, The Brilliant World of Tom Gates, for whole story.)

Mr Keen thinks I'm upset at missing the school concert.

Oh dear.
sniff sniff

(I'm **not**.)

I hold my bag up to my face and try to sneak past him. Despite me using small children for extra cover ... he sees me.

 "TOM!"

(Keep walking, keep walking...)

"TOM GATES! Just the person I was looking for!"

(Too late.)

"Yes, Mr Keen."

"I see you're in a BAND with Derek Fingle?"

(How did he know that?)

"And you're looking for a NEW drummer?"

For a TERRIBLE moment I think Mr Keen wants to join our band until he says,

"Very good poster, by the way."

Phew.

(Derek must have put the poster up yesterday.)

"I know how disappointed you were to miss out on performing in the school concert."

"No, no..."

He ignores me.

Mr Keen then tells me that Mr Sprocket

(our music teacher) has put together a

SPECIAL SCHOOL BAND

that will be performing in a very important

assembly. And GUESS WHAT? Thanks to Mr

Keen, Derek and I are IN the school band NOW.

"Isn't that exciting, Tom?"

I'm lost for words.

"What instrument does Derek play, Tom?"

"Keyboards, Mr Keen ... but I don't think—"
Too late - Mr Keen has already gone.
Derek won't be happy.

Oh no...

I don't even know what kind of music the school band plays.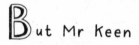

I suppose it might be OK? (Extra band practice for **DOGZOMBIES** at least.)

But Mr Keen has reminded me about the

BAND
AUDITION
POSTER

I can't wait to find out WHO wants to be in our band!

On the way to class I go and take a quick look at the poster.

☉ ☉ Mmmmmmmmmmmmm.

(Oh...)

I'm not sure everyone is taking this very seriously.

Hang on ...
AMY PORTER

has added her name!

That's a surprise.

Amy is obviously taking **DOGZOMBIES** very seriously. Because she is super smart with excellent taste in music. I'll tell Derek the news like this:

"YEAH! GOOD NEWS! ☺

Amy Porter is auditioning for the band.

BOO! BAD NEWS. ☹

Mr Keen has put US in the SCHOOL BAND."

(I'll say the bad news bit really fast ... he might not notice.)

In class, Mr Fullerman asks about my tooth.

How's your tooth, Tom?

So I hand over my

→ REAL ←

sick note...

Dear Mr Fullerman,

Please could Tom be excused from PE
just for ~~the week~~ the week as he has a VERY SERIOUS nasty tooth

infection which has almost cleared up.

Kind regards,

Rita Gates

Mr Fullerman reads it carefully.

(I hope he doesn't spot my "changes".)

So far so good.

Then he gives me a L O N G →
list of work 😟 to catch up on.

I tell Mr Fullerman this <u>MUST</u> be a mistake
because I was only away for one day. Amy
says, "You missed loads."

Great.

Now I'm wondering if this is a good time 🙂
to mention the DOGZOMBIES audition poster
that Amy signed up for. I could give her a few
tips?

(Like "Bring caramel wafers".)

But Mr Fullerman interrupts. He tells us about the **"really exciting school field trip I have planned"**.

(Sounds like fun.)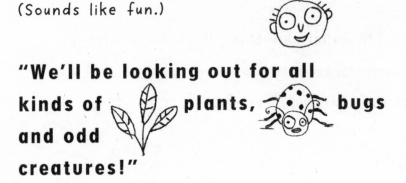

"We'll be looking out for all kinds of plants, bugs and odd creatures!"

I nudge Amy and point to Marcus...

"Found one."

Odd Creature

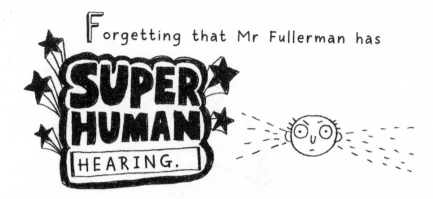

Forgetting that Mr Fullerman has **SUPER HUMAN HEARING.**

He gives me a teacher stare and says,

"TOM, along with finding odd creatures, I'll be expecting YOU to tell us LOTS of interesting information about trees, as it seems you're a bit of an expert."

Which shuts me up.

I have NO idea why Mr Fullerman thinks I'm an expert on trees.

THIS would be my idea of an INTERESTING TREE.

Next **Mr Fullerman** hands out more

homework ... groan.

Class 5F Homework
From: Mr Fullerman
Oakfield School

Dear Class 5F

This week I want you to write a proper
thank-you letter.
You need to decide who you're writing to
and what you are thanking them for.
Was it a present or perhaps some good
advice?
Use your imagination.
Describe how you feel and remember to lay
out the letter correctly.
Looking forward to reading your letters.
Kind regards

Mr Fullerman

The homework could be worse, I suppose. At least it's **not** fractions or anything really tricky like that.

How hard is it to say

THANK YOU?

Unless it's to Delia.

But that **NEVER** happens.

At home time Derek and I are busy discussing Who has signed our

DOGZOMBIES audition poster.

So far it's only Amy,

Florence
and
NORMAN.

I'm guessing SUPERMAN

and MICKEY MOUSE

won't turn up.

I remember to tell Derek that Mr Keen might want to talk to him about being in the school band.

"I'll just say NO thanks, Sir."

"Too Late ... we're in the school band."

"At least he doesn't know I play keyboard," Derek says.

"...he might now.

(It just slipped out, sorry.)"

Derek is wondering what exactly Mr Keen is planning, when Marcus runs past

REALLY fast.

He says "Move move" and pushes us aside. I notice Marcus has lost the limp caused by the terrible SCAR from his **ENORMOUS** new dog.

"What's the hurry?" I say, but he's already gone.

Derek says, "Let's follow him outside and see what he's up to."

"OK."

Marcus has ⸺ rushed over to his dad, who's in the car waiting. We watch Marcus open the door and ⫽ l e a n inside, like he's trying to reach something.

Here, boy.

Derek says, "I can hear BARKING!"

"So can I."

"**It** <u>must</u> be his new dog!"

"**T**he one that BIT him!" I say.

Grrr

We can't see 👀 the dog yet but his BARK

is VERY **LOUD**.

Marcus is holding a dog lead and being pulled
around.

"Maybe Marcus has a **FIERCE** dog
after all?" Derek says.

"From the way he's struggling to control it, his
dog must be really **BIG**

and **STRONG**," I say...

...or maybe not.

Grrrrrrrrrr

HOMEWORK

Ever since **Mr Fullerman** sent that letter home about my **ReVIEW HOMEWORK**, Mum is being tough on me.

> Homework first, dinner after, Tom.

But it's difficult to concentrate because I keep thinking about:

1. Marcus being dragged along by his teeny weeny dog. **Hilarious!**

2. Dinner.

3. Dinner.

4. The DOGZOMBIE drummer auditions.

It's excellent news that Amy Porter has put her name down. She's so SUPER SMART at EVERYTHING. I can't wait to see how good she is at drumming.

I think this

could work.

We are holding the auditions
in Derek's garage at the weekend.
Derek's dad, Mr Fingle, has been BANNED.

Everyone who turns up will have a chance to audition, even if they're rubbish.
As well as the audition, I'm ALSO thinking about...

5. Dad's birthday, which is <u>really</u>

soon. What to get him?

-Draw a picture?

-Chocolates?

 -Socks

- New hat?

Mum told Aunty Alice

that she had

already arranged
a little get-together

for Dad to avoid having a party

like last year.

surprise

Now EVERYONE is coming round to ours.

Including Granny and Granddad Gates,

or THE FOSSILS as I like to call them,

because they are very

old and ancient.

Which has just given me a GREAT idea

for my THANK YOU letter homework. Genius ...

thanks, Fossils.

Dear Granny,

THANK YOU

FOR THE

POCKET

MONEY.

Love, Tom

(YOUR FAVOURITE GRANDSON.) x x

Tom,

I have no doubt you are a wonderful grandson.

But I need to see a much longer thank-you letter next time, please.

1 merit.

But well done for joining the NEW SCHOOL BAND. Mr Keen was extremely pleased.

Mr Fullerman

Great, now it's official.

Written in black and white by
Mr Fullerman that I AM
in the school band.

I'm guessing he wasn't impressed with my

letter.

And I only got one merit. Which is
a bit **harsh**, I think?

Maybe this might help...

To: Mr Fullerman

Let me explain about the slightly small
thank-you letter.
My granny is VERY OLD with dodgy
eyes ☉ ☉ and she falls asleep a <u>lot.</u>
So a thank-you letter needs to be in
REALLY BIG WRITING and
VERY VERY SHORT. Or she can't read
it. (I am a thoughtful grandson ...
it's true.) ☺

From: Tom Gates
　　　　↖(<u>Hard</u>-working pupil who
deserves a few more merits, maybe?)

Space left for EXTRA

merits ... is still empty.

Oh well, worth a try.

Over the next few days Mr Fullerman reminds everyone in class that...

"REALLY hard-working pupils get the extra merits."

(OK, point taken.)

So I'm doing some EXTRA reading at home when Granny and Granddad pop in for a cup of tea.

I can hear them chit-chatting

Chit

Chat

downstairs with Dad.

I go to say hello (and sneak a biscuit).

Tea + Fossils = BISCUITS

But Dad spots me and says, "No biscuits for you until your tooth infection has cleared up."

J ust then Delia comes in and hears
the word "INFECTION".

"Ugh ... disgusting. What's he got now?"
Delia is leaning away from me like
I have THE LURGY while helping
herself to a biscuit. Right in
front of me, too!

"That's not FAIR,"
I say.

"Delia hasn't got a bad tooth like you,"
Dad says.

"Ugh, he's Rotting," she

laughs, holding her nose.

Granddad says that I **MUST** take care of
my teeth or I'll end up looking
like him.

Then he says, "Do you want to see what
happens to you if you DON'T look after
your teeth?"

Granny tries to stop him.

"Don't show him, **Bob**... It's not nice."

Now I'm *REALLY* curious.

"Your teeth look fine to me, Granddad."

That's when he turns his back ...

and takes his teeth OUT of his mouth!

It's HILARIOUS!

Now he's got them IN HIS HAND. (OK, that looks weird.)

"See ... no teeeffff leffft."
Granddad's mouth reminds me of a very old turtle.

Delia says, "...that's rank."
Granny tells Granddad to put them back and "don't be so childish."

Which doesn't stop Granddad from
pretending to BITE Granny
before slipping his teeth back
into his mouth. (They make a
strange clunking sound as they settle down.)

CLUNK!

Granny tries to change the subject
(well, sort of).

She's MADE her | own | biscuits.

Uh oh.

"They are **packed** full of nuts, honey and all kinds of other LOVELY stuff," she says.

Granny Mavis has very weird taste in food. So "other lovely stuff" could really be ANYTHING.

Here are a couple of her favourite "specials".

La La
La

Granny's cheese and jam sandwiches?

Why?

CHOC

Grated chocolate on pasta...

Dad says I'm allowed a home-made biscuit if I promise to brush my teeth afterwards.

Granny arranges her "biscuits" on a plate and says, "Tuck in!"

But her biscuits look a bit like...

FISH?

(Oh dear.)

"They're not fish flavoured!" Granny assures me.

Phew. But they do have **BIG** stary eyes.
(I risk it ... for a biscuit.)

Mmmmmm, surprisingly tasty for a
fish biscuit.
The eyes are a bit crunchy, though.

Delia's already left (after Granddad's teeth
trick) so there are more biscuits for me. When
Dad's not looking I sneak a couple for later.

 REsuLT!

While the Fossils are still here, Mum
remembers to invite them to Dad's
birthday party.

Dad is still not keen on having a party at ALL after last year.

I did it MY way

So while he's grumbling and complaining, I remind everyone that it's MY birthday soon. And I'm VERY keen to have a

PARTY with presents.

Granddad wonders what I'm interested in these days.

(Perfect time to drop "present hints".)

I am about to say **DUDE 3** electric
guitars, drawing stuff, that kind of thing.

When Mum **BUTTS** in with
"Tom's REALLY interested in trees,
aren't you, Tom?"
I am?

"Remember the wonderful
piece of homework you did
on trees?"

Errrrrrrr. BLANK.

I decide to take the praise while it's being
handed to me because:

Good schoolwork + Birthday = Extra good presents

But just in case I say...

" 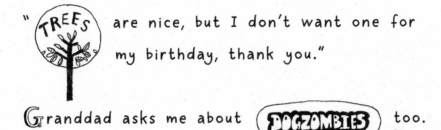 are nice, but I don't want one for my birthday, thank you."

Granddad asks me about DOGZOMBIES too.

(I'm very impressed he remembered my band's name!)

He says he has the PERFECT venue for us to play our VERY FIRST GIG ... when we're ready.

"This place is always looking for new acts," Granddad says.

"Really?"

"Yes, you'll have a big audience of friendly people."

W⊙W, EXCELLENT! I can't wait to tell Derek. Then Granny offers me another biscuit, so I take it (to go with the other two I already have).

I have LOTS of good stuff to chat about with Derek now.

☺ FIRST EVER DOGZOMBIES GIG

☺ FISH BISCUITS

☺ GRANDDAD'S TEETH

Round at Derek's house, he is STILL not very happy about being in the school band.

So I give him the TWO fish biscuits, which makes him laugh.

"Your granny's weird," he says, looking at the biscuit ⊙ ⊙ eyes.

"But they taste nice, though," he adds. ☺

I'm telling Derek how THE FOSSILS are not always that bonkers and sometimes

they're REALLY funny.

"Mostly they are just like really ordinary grandparents, honestly."

Derek says, "Are you sure about that?"

OK, maybe Derek has a point.

Mr Fullerman

... is doing that teacher thing of *leaning* on his desk Staring at everyone.

He says he has got some very IMPORTANT news for us all.

(His idea of what's important is different to mine.)

F or instance ... **DOGZOMBIES** band auditions are important. I'm still not sure if I should say anything to **AMY** about them. I decide not to.

Not the right time. I notice that she's holding her pencil and tapping it on the desk (which is the sort of thing a drummer would do).

 It's a good sign. ☺

While I have been studying **AMY's** drumming, Mr Fullerman has gone ahead and made his

"IMPORTANT ANNOUNCEMENT".

I've missed it. Oh well.

$\mathbb{B}$ut then he asks me a question.

"Isn't that right ... Tom?"

(This is why I prefer being at the of the classroom, not at the front.)

I have N⊙ idea what Mr Fullerman is talking about, so I just agree with him.

Yes, Mr Fullerman.

"Great, well done Tom. Does anyone else want to go too?"

Huh?

"No ... OK, looks like it's just you, Tom. And Derek too. Off you go. You'll be the first on the chart."

WHAT? THE FIRST? I have a horrible feeling about this. Well, at least I get to miss a lesson (I think?).

GOLD STAR AWARD CHART
CLASS 5F

MARK CLUMP	ROSS WHITE
BRAD GALLOWAY	SOLOMAN STEWART
TOM GATES	PANSY BENNET
PAUL JOLLY	INDRANI HINDLE
LEROY LEWIS	FLORENCE MITCHELL
MARCUS MELDREW	JULIA MORTON
TREVOR PETERS	AMY PORTER
NORMAN WATSON	AMBER TULLEY GREEN

The GOOD NEWS is, I've got the

FIRST GOLD ⭐ STAR on the new

Award Chart. Mr Fullerman has given

me a star for joining the school band. (Like I

had a choice?)

Which is unexpected but nice.

The BAD news is, school band practice

is on NOW and I have to go on my

own. 😞 Oh well, at least I'm missing maths

lessons in class.

Question: How bad can a school band

really be?

Answer: Worse than I thought.

Mr Sprocket is delighted to see us.

Derek and I are ‎ not ‎ so delighted.

"Let me explain," Mr Sprocket tells us. "This school band is different. We use recycled rubbish made into instruments.

We play new modern music too."

(Which just means no one has ever heard of
it.)
"Not exactly DOGZOMBIES, is it?" I whisper to
Derek.

Parr

Mr Sprocket asks us to choose an "instrument". As there are NO guitars or keyboards I pick the plastic-bottle-looking thing with chopsticks. Derek goes for the wooden box with elastic bands.

We do the best we can under the circumstances.

When I hit the bottles they are supposed to make different notes.

So far, mine only have two notes.

CLANG! and even LOUDER CLANG!

The other kids are more practised than us – they are making it look easy (it's not!).

We keep making mistakes.

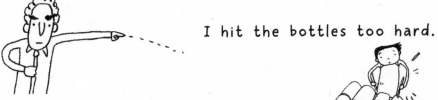

I hit the bottles too hard.

Derek has pinged quite a few of his elastic bands. PING

Then I break a chopstick and half of it flies through the air.

School band is not going well.

Even Mr Sprocket looks a little weary.

One kid puts his hand up.

"Sir, why are they in our band?"

"OUR BAND"? I thought it was a school band?
Mr Sprocket tells him to put his hand down because we'll be fine,

after one or two more rehearsals.

"More like one or two HUNDRED."

Ha! Ha! Ha!

I can hear more kids laughing now.
I'm going to HAVE to think of a really EXCELLENT excuse to get out of this band.
It's been an Awful practice.

$\mathbb{D}$erek agrees. "That was embarrassing," he says.

Then I notice where the other half of my chopstick has landed.
I nudge Derek. "No, THAT'S embarrassing."
Mr Sprocket looks like he has a bow in his hair.
We leave quickly, before he notices.

Whoops

Outside the classroom, Amy and Florence are walking past.
"Is this your new band, Tom?" Amy asks.
"No way," I say. "This is the school band. It's a bit rubbish, really." The kids in the school band hear me and are not happy. 😞

"We're not rubbish. YOU'RE the one who's rubbish."

"And so's your friend."

"We'd be ten times better if you weren't in the school band."
(They have a point.)

GREAT. Now Amy and Florence think that we're hopeless. I'm just about to EXPLAIN to them that we play

REAL instruments in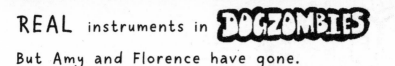

But Amy and Florence have gone.

"This **school band** could RUIN our reputation ... if we had one," Derek says.

It's true.

Today we've been a bit:

⇨ RUBBISH

⇨ SHAMED

and ⟹ EMBARRASSED.

Derek and I decide we have to get out of the school band, one way or another.

It's the most important thing to do ever.

Until I find a spare wafer in my pocket.

Share a wafer?

YES

YEAH!

The poster has been up for a few days and we're doing the auditions TOMORROW, so I am very excited to see ⊙ ⊙ who else has added their names to the list.

Let me see...

HANG ON!

Amy Porter

AND

FLORENCE MITCHELL'S

names have been CROSSED OUT?

What's going on? Who's done that?

So far the only *REAL* person who's coming to the audition is: HYPERACTIVE

NORMAN WATSON.

I take down the poster and go and find Amy *quickly.*

Stan the school caretaker is holding open
the door for some kids. I can see ⊙ ⊙ Amy
and Florence in front of me. So I
≡R U S H past everyone, saying,

"EMERGENCY!

EMERGENCY!

EMERGENCY!"

Which gets their attention.

I catch up with Amy and Florence and show them the poster.

"LOOK at what

SOMEBODY

HAS done!

Can you believe they've actually CROSSED

BOTH your names OFF from the

audition! What kind of an IDIOT would

ruin your chances of being in DOGZOMBIES

by doing something as STUPID

as that ?"

Then Amy says,

It was me.

(Oh ... I wasn't expecting that.)

Florence says, "We don't play drums, Tom."

"And we didn't write our names on your poster. Sorry," Amy adds.

"Does that mean you won't be auditioning, then?" Just checking.

No, Tom.

Caretaker Stan is listening to our conversation.

"**H**ey! Looking for a drummer? Well, look

no further!"

Stan thinks he's funny. Groan.

He pretends to do a drum

roll and cymbal crash.

(Which is rubbish.)

The door slowly closes while

Stan continues to air drum.

I'm trying not to look fed up.

"**Y**ou wouldn't want us in your band, Tom,"

Florence says.

"**W**e'd be ROTTEN," Amy adds.

"Worse than Stan?" I say.

(We can still hear Stan's keys jangling in the

background.)

Amy suspects whoever wrote the Silly names on the poster also wrote their names on it too.

Good point.

"See if you can match the handwriting on the poster to anyone in our class," Amy suggests.

"That's genius!" I say. (She's so smart.)

Whoever wanted to mess up the audition poster is probably feeling pretty pleased with themselves right now.

I'm searching the classroom for ANYONE who seems slightly more smug than usual...

mmmmm

Extreme close up

Surprise, surprise...

It **WAS** Marcus who wrote on the poster. He admits it.

He says, "You didn't actually think Amy and Florence wanted to be in your band, did you?" Ha! Ha! Ha! he laughs. (He's so annoying.)

Mr Fullerman has marked all our REVIEW homework and is handing them back to us.

"Well done, Tom, excellent work," he says.

Marcus doesn't get a mention.

☺

(I did my homework quickly, so this is very good news.)

Good work, Tom.

Your special interest in trees will be very useful on the field trip.

Well Done

3 merits and ONE GOLD STAR.

THAT'S why Mr Fullerman thought I was interested in TREES.

I'll show this to Mum and Dad, who might give me a REWARD.

Cake REWARD

REWARD BISCUITS

CHOCOLATE REWARD

FIZZY REWARD

Cash Reward

I could try the "good parenting" line again?
Worth a go... ☺

Right now I enjoy collecting my

SECOND GOLD ⭐

2 merits = 1 GOLD STAR.

Whoever gets the MOST stars at the end
of the term wins "spectacular prizes". (So Mr
Fullerman tells us.)

I suspect the prizes will be things
like pencil cases and school
tea towels.

OAKFIELD SCHOOL

NOT very spectacular at all.

But as I am in the lead with two stars ... I
don't care.
I leave my book open so MARCUS can see my

MERITS

AND → GOLD STARS

Sadly, nobody else (REAL) has put their names down for our audition.

Looks like it's ONLY NORMAN coming now. I don't think his audition will take too long.

Derek hopes someone else will turn up ... other than just his dad. Who keeps popping in.

Anyone here yet?

Derek sends him away.

I remind Derek that my granddad has

already booked **DOGZOMBIES'** FIRST EVER GIG!

"We can still do it, even if we don't have a drummer," I say.

(That's plan B, in case no one turns up.)

"Granddad says we'll be in front of a nice friendly crowd."

"BRILLIANT." Derek is trying to be positive.

"We could become the NEXT **DUDE 3**," I say. How cool would that be?

Then Norman turns up, which brings us right back down to earth.

He's being his usual **TWITCHY** self.

"Hey, Norman, just relax and play anything you want to," I tell him.

Whoops!

(We're not expecting too much from him.)

"Bit nervous," he says as he knocks over another drum.

It's not a great start.

The noise gives Derek's dad an excuse to COME in AGAIN to see what we're getting up to (like he doesn't already know).

I'm really hoping that Norman's drumming is better than his swimming ... but so far, it's not looking good.

Norman settles down (a bit).

Then he starts to play.

Need any help?

And we're all in for a MASSIVE SURPRISE...

☆ NORMAN is AMAZING! ☆

OK, he is a bit wild...

When he's finished playing, we tell Norman
he's "IN THE BAND!" Which sets him off again.

Norman is much better at playing than we are.
"We might have to practise more,"

I say to Derek.

"You'll sound like a proper band with
Norman drumming!" Mr Fingle tells us.

Then he adds...

Talking of PROPER bands.

(Uh oh.) We haven't had a chance to

WARN Norman about

Mr Fingle's little

CHATS.

He's already rummaging in his record collection.

"Have you ever heard of a band called

THE WHO, Norman?"

"Who?" Norman says.

"NO, THE WHO,"

Mr Fingle repeats.

Then Norman asks, "Who are The Who, then?"

Which is really confusing.

Derek wants his dad to STOP chatting.

"Not now, Dad, PLEASE!"

(But it's too late.)

"Only one of the BEST BANDS

in the whole world ever!" he says as he proudly

shows Norman the record.

"This is a CLASSIC,

you must listen to it ...

right NOW!"

Norman says, "OK, sure!"

Then jumps up just a little bit too quickly to

take a look at the album.

The record flies HIGH in the air, out of its sleeve, then lands on the ground.

It rolls across the floor,

spins a bit, then

through some.: dust,

comes to a stop.

Mr Fingle is FREAKING out that his record has been SCRATCHED and ruined.

"Don't PANIC,

I'll FETCH IT!" he shouts.

Really REALLY LOUDLY.

SO loudly that Rooster (Derek's dog) hears the word FETCH and

runs in from the

garden. He grabs the record in his teeth, then disappears out of the door. Followed quickly by Mr Fingle.

Derek says he's never seen his dad run so fast.

"It must be a really good album," Norman says.

"And Rooster has very good taste in music," I add.

The audition is over now, so we watch Mr Fingle chase Rooster all around the house.

When I get home,
this letter from my school
has turned up.

From: Oakfield School

To: Mr and Mrs Gates
24 Castle St
EGP 1963

I'm wondering WHAT I've done NOW? So I open
it carefully and take a sneaky look. ☉ ☉

£PHEW!}   Just a reminder about the
                 school field trip and a
special ➡ <u>Clothes List.</u>

                 (Nothing important, then.)

FIELD TRIP

I'm LATE

for the field trip due to:

1. Forgetting about the field trip.

2. Forgetting I still had my pyjama

bottoms on as I left for school.

I run back to get changed.

Delia sees me and is her usual

helpful self.

FOOL.

I only just make it to school on time.

LATE AGAIN, TOM?

Mr Fullerman and the whole class are

waiting for me outside. For some strange

reason Mr Fullerman is dressed like a

jungle explorer?

226

Solid is there and wearing very impressive waterproof boots.

I ask him if Mr Fullerman is looking for BUGS or TIGERS?

He laughs loudly and Mr Fullerman STARES at me ... then at my feet. (Uh oh.)

Apparently I'm wearing

inappropriate footwear

And I might have to wear the

SPARE BOOTS!

(NOT the SPARE BOOTS.

No! No!)

The "SPARE" stuff is mostly MANKY bits of lost property that no one wants (like this).

Spare T-shirt.

Spare shorts.

(I hope he forgets about my shoes.)

MRS Mumble is on the trip with us. She's holding the bag of "spare stuff".

"For emergencies," she tells me cheerily.

"Or people with inappropriate footwear," Marcus adds.

I ignore him.

Norman is still very overexcited about being in DOGZOMBIES.

He keeps jumping around and using his magnifying glass to LOOM

up to people with one big EYE.
(It's getting on everyone's nerves.)

Marcus is getting on my nerves.

"Didn't you read the field trip clothes list?" he asks me. "SHHHHH," I say.

It will be ALL Marcus's fault if I have to wear the SPARE BOOTS.

Mr Fullerman gets distracted when Norman looms up to Julia Morton once too often.

AGH!

We all have to "PAY ATTENTION" to the
safety talk about things that could

STING ⊖

and

BITE.

**"You must behave
SENSIBLY."**

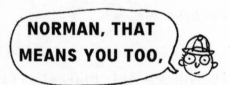

NORMAN, THAT
MEANS YOU TOO,

Mr Fullerman says.

We set off with Mr Fullerman at the front
and Mrs Mumble at the back to make sure no
one dawdles behind.

Don't dawdle

We're not going far, just to the local field.

When we get there we are put into groups and have to go off and identify as many different types of plants, leaves and TREES as we can.

"You should be good at this, Tom, you know a lot about trees," Mr Fullerman says.

Great, now my group think I'm some kind of WEIRD TREE EXPERT (I'm not).

Instead I just make stuff up, which seems to work.

Here we have the lesser spotted tree.

I'm really looking forward to using the BUG CATCHERS we've been given.

Pansy Bennet has already found an

ENORMOUS spider.

Leroy Lewis is studying a bug that

ROLLS up in a ball.

Mark Clump is catching EVERYTHING.

Ants, bugs, spiders, frogs – the lot.

I spot a really brightly coloured beetle. I've never seen one like that before.

CLOSE UP!

I sneak up really slowly. THIS bug looks AMAZING, I might even get THREE merits (and one GOLD ☆) for discovering it.

I lower my bug catcher over the bug carefully...

Easy does it...

Marcus suddenly

traps it in **HIS** bug catcher.

"THAT'S MINE," he says.

(I really hope it bites him or stings him ... or both.)

Irritating or what?

Florence and Amy come over
to show me what they have found.
GRASSHOPPERS, which are very cool.
(It takes my mind off Marcus.)

Amy wonders how the audition

went "with ONLY Norman turning up?"

"He was BRILLIANT," I say.

"Really?" Florence doesn't sound convinced.

"Aren't you worried about Norman being in the band?" Amy asks.

"No, not really," I say. "Norman can be a bit, you know..."

"Bonkers," Florence adds.

So I tell them.

"You'd be surprised. Norman's actually a REALLY GREAT drummer."

"What about all the crazy things he does?" Amy says.

"Norman's not THAT bad. Honestly, when was the last time you saw him do something REALLY silly?" I add.

Just as Norman turns up holding

TWO green caterpillars

under his nose.

"LOOK ...
BOGEYS!"

(Not now, Norman ... groan.)

We are sitting on the grass eating our
packed lunches when SOLID (who looks
a bit miserable) shows me the only thing he's
found so far.

I think 👁 👁 it's half a dead bug ...
it [is] half a dead bug.

half bug

"I'll help you find something else,"
I say.

So Solid FLICKS the dead bug away.

(Which probably wasn't the best idea.)

The bug flies through the air and lands right on Julia Morton's sandwich.

Julia SCREAMS and says she feels sick now.

Mrs Mumble assures her that the bug probably fell from the tree.

(Me and Solid keep quiet.)

Unlike MARCUS, who tells Julia that there is a very good reason she has only HALF a dead bug on her sandwich.

"What's that, then?" Julia asks.

"You must have EATEN the other half already."

The whole class go "UGGGGHHHHHHHhh!"

Julia turns green. (She's the same colour as the grass now.)

Marcus is laughing and being particularly irritating today.

Mr Fullerman tells everyone to "Calm down!"

He lets Julia "recover" by sitting under a tree. Then takes the rest of the class down to the pond to carry on looking for creatures.

OK, now I see why I needed to wear boots. A SOLID has already

SUNK down into the mUD

and has to be pulled out by Mrs Mumble. (Who's a LOT stronger than she looks.) ◌ ◌

Mrs Mumble tells me to keep clear of the mUD "in those shoes".

Then Marcus adds

"He should be wearing the SPARE BOOTS,

Mrs Mumble."

SHUT UP, MARCUS! I wish he'd sink down in the mud.

Mr Fullerman calls us all over to see what he's been collecting in the bucket. Amongst all the SLIME and WEEDS are some tiny little and other interesting things.

"Take turns to look ... don't push,"

Mr Fullerman says.

(Marcus is pushing now.) It's tricky to see exactly what's in there. SOLID thinks he

saw a "WATER SNAKE!"

"You can all see ... be patient," Mr Fullerman tells us.

Then he asks Mark Clump and Amber Tulley Green to help carry the bucket up the grass.

Norman's not great at being patient and can't wait. He hears Solid say "WATER SNAKE" and gets really excited. Then accidentally *T R I P S* over a twig and falls on Amber.

Who lets go of the bucket.
Mark Clump holds on with one hand.
Until a BIG FROG

POPS out of his pocket. (He'd forgotten about the frog.)

It *LEAPS OUT*

and Mark tries to catch it (again).

Rivvett!

Mark lets go of the bucket.

The bucket goes FLYING UP in the air

and all the tiny

fish, weeds and slime

spill out

EVERYWHERE.

ALL OVER **MARCUS**.

(Turns out there wasn't a water snake in the bucket after all. Just lots and lots of slime.) Marcus is not happy. Solid has cheered up, though. Mrs Mumble comes to the rescue with a towel. She says:

"Don't panic, I've got just the thing for this kind of

EMERGENCY."

Mr Fullerman and the rest of the class scoop up any fish or creatures from the ground and take them back to the pond, while Mrs Mumble helps Marcus.

She says...

"Thank GOODNESS we brought the SPARE CLOTHES ...

and the SPARE BOOTS!"

(I agree.)

Marcus has to wear them all the way back

to school. Which **inspires** me to draw
some of the bugs and creatures I COULD HAVE
found on the field trip.

Worth at least five merits, I think?

Dad's Birthday

Everyone's coming to our house for Dad's birthday party, which means Mum is a LOT more stressed than usual. She keeps saying things like

"Take it upstairs!" and
"Rubbish outside!"

Delia thinks it's funny to try and put ME outside.

Mum gets CROSS

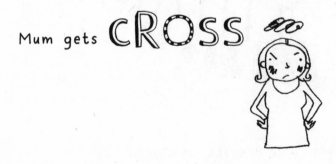

and says that we had **BOTH** better behave
when guests arrive

or else!

The whole house is all

CLEAN and TIDY.

Until the Fingles turn up early
with their dog Rooster.
He's got really muddy paws.

Garden!

Rooster isn't in the house
for very long thanks to
Mum.

Derek gives **D**ad his present. (I can guess what it is from its shape.) 😊

Dad's DELIGHTED. He's already discussing with Mr Fingle "classic albums" and "great bands of our day".

(Yawn.)

It's not biscuits.

I give **D**ad my present before he gets too carried away chatting.

It's a T-shirt with my drawing on the front.

TOM GATES

Dad LOVES it!

He says I've gone to a ⟨LOT⟩ of trouble.

Actually it was Mum who put it on a T-shirt.

But I'm happy to take the praise.

Thank you. Thank you.

Dad wants to wear it straight away.

"IT FITS..." Mum says because she

thought it might be a bit snug.

(Which doesn't go down well with Dad.)

Derek says that DOGZOMBIES should have

T-shirts too. Which is an

EXCELLENT idea.

When Uncle Kevin, Aunty Alice and the cousins turn up, they are all wearing

VERY *fancy* clothes.

Dad wonders if they are going to another party afterwards?

Uncle Kevin says, "It's important to make an effort when you're invited out."

(He's looking at Dad like he's a bit scruffy.)

So Dad tells him that I made the T-shirt as a present.

"Tom's so talented, isn't it great?"

Which makes Delia do "I'm going to be sick" signs behind Dad's back.

I ignore her and AGREE with Dad, that I am a GENIUS ... it's true.

Uncle Kevin says, "Well done, Tom."

And Dad's happy ...

... until Aunty Alice gives him their present.

251

It's a book called

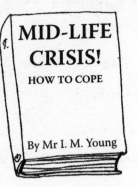

Uncle Kevin says,

MID-LIFE
CRISIS!
HOW TO COPE

By Mr I. M. Young

"We saw this and
thought of you."

Aunty Alice adds, "It was recommended for men of your age."

Dad says "Thanks!" but he doesn't look

THAT pleased.

THE FOSSILS arrive in their usual

STYLE. Granny

has brought one of her cakes

(well, I think it's a cake; you

never know with Granny).

I'm guessing Delia **FORGOT**

to buy Dad a present.

Because she's just given him ...

a pair of her **OLD**

sunglasses?

Dad puts them on and says, "Thanks, Delia, I look `JUST` like you now!"

Which is not really true

because Dad is SMILING.

Mum tells me I have to

look after Derek and
your cousins

(this means "keep out of trouble").

Everything's going well

until all the good snacks

run out.

Then the cousins announce that

they have brought over

so we can ALL finish watching it. ⊙ ⊙

"Let's watch it NOW,"

they say.

(Let's not.)

Derek looks keen to see it but I want to avoid

hiding behind cushions AGAIN.

QUICKLY I suggest, "We
should play a few jokes
instead."

Which turns out to be a BRILLIANT IDEA.

ha
ha

The whoopee cushion works well on Delia. And Aunty Alice too.

parp

parp

whoopee cushion

Putting me inside a LARGE box as an "EXTRA present" for Dad was INSPIRED.

TO
DAD
xx

I SPRING out shouting

SURPRISE

Dad laughs but Uncle Kevin's not smiling much, because I've accidentally

262

knocked a bowl of crisps all over his
fancy bow tie.

Mum **AND** Uncle Kevin are GLARING at

me. When Granny comes to my rescue by
bringing in Dad's birthday cake.

...Which is slightly

unusual?

"It's a delicious

vegetable

cake," she says.

(Mmmm it doesn't look so delicious to me?)

We all sing "HAPPY BIRTHDAY"
to Dad.

(This is my version that I made up.)

"Happy birthday to you
You're a hundred and two
You've lost all your hair now
and your teeth are brand new!" ☺

Dad blows out his candles and calls me a "cheeky monkey".

Uncle Kevin jokes that if we run out of breath we might need a fire extinguisher for all those candles. Ha. Ha.

The cousins tuck into the cake first. (No surprise there.)

It MUST taste better than it looks.

Then Granddad wants to REMIND us that **DOGZOMBIES** are playing our

VERY *first* gig on Sunday...

WE ARE?

"This Sunday?

That's a bit soon, isn't it?" I say.

Granddad says it's all booked. So we'd better get practising. Which is a good point because we still only know a few songs.

"**B**esides, if you don't come and play, I'll be **FORCED** to entertain everyone with my ◯NE │ VERY │ special party trick," Granddad tells us.

Derek wants to know what

his *Party Trick* │ actually │ is.

(I'm not sure what it is either.)

Teeth

OK,

        just remembered.

Meanwhile... The cousins | STILL | want
me to see the film. 👀
(I'd rather watch Granddad take his teeth out
again.) But it's too late, they are sitting in
front of the TV waiting for me to join them.

MYSTERIOUSLY ... the remote control
goes (MISSING.)

(I've hidden it.)

Remote
control is
MISSING

I tell them that the TV is **STUCK**
on this channel. Which is showing a programme
on ... VAMPIRES. (That's lucky.)

I leave them to it. The cousins
are VERY happy until Aunty
Alice and Uncle Kevin come to take them home.

Which turns out to be a **lot** sooner

 than expected due to Uncle Kevin

hurting his back. "I knew dancing was

a mistake," he says.

Dad says Uncle Kevin is

Not like the **FOSSILS,** who are

having a great time making everyone join in

their CONGA line. They dance all around the

house and into the garden too. It's slightly

embarrassing (but fun).

At least Dad looks like he's enjoying himself

this year.

Unlike Delia.

The Special ASSEMBLY

Get this...

Derek is off school today because he's sprained his ankle 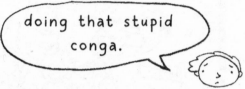 doing that stupid conga.

I have to go in on my own, which is FINE until I get to school and overhear Mr Keen talking to Mr Fullerman about the

SPECIAL ASSEMBLY.

OH! NO! What with Dad's birthday and everything, I have completely forgotten all about the *special assembly* and playing in the school band!

(DEREK picked a good day for a dodgy ankle.)

I'm trying to avoid Mr Keen **AGAIN**, until I can think of an EXCELLENT excuse to get myself **OUT** of this sticky situation.

It's bad enough playing "instruments" (bottles with chopsticks). But doing it without Derek will be too embarrassing for me.

What to do?

I walk very *SLOWLY* into class to give myself time to think.

Marcus is walking in front of me. He starts **LIMPING** when he sees me.

"The dog bite scar?"

Marcus says. "It still hurts." This gives me an idea. ☺

(Thanks, Marcus, for a change.)

DISASTER! I am STRUCK

DOWN with a terrible DEAD ARM ache...

Mr Fullerman wonders how this could have happened SO suddenly?

I explain how my older sister DELIA pushed me out of the house and how she MUST have sprained my "instrument-playing arm VERY badly".

"It's AGONY," I say.

I do some extra VERY LOUD groaning during registration, which I think helps. Mr Fullerman sends me to the medical room - again.

I moan a bit more (OK, a lot more, for extra effect on the way out).

 Mrs Mumble tells me to sit in the medical room and wait for a bit.

Medical Room

UNFORTUNATELY

I miss **ALL** of the special assembly [and] playing in the school band too.

RESULT!

Once everything is safely over, I make a remarkable recovery.

My arm is fine now

... see.

Tah dah!

It's a MIRACLE.

It's safe to go back to class.

I just have to avoid Mr Keen for the rest of the day, which I manage to do with the help of:

Doors.

Walls.

And SOLID.

I can't avoid Mr Fullerman, though. He calls me over for a **"quick chat"**. (I think he's slightly suspicious about my instant recovery from arm ache.)

Mr Fullerman says,

"Such a shame you missed the special assembly, Tom."

(Not really.)

"Glad your arm is better ... so quickly, too?"

(Uh oh.)

I tell Mr Fullerman my arm feels absolutely FINE now. And THAT'S when I notice

the book under Mr Fullerman's arm.

IT's a book on TREES.

(Which looks VERY familiar?)

Mr Fullerman hands me back my

REVIEW HOMEWORK.

The one I did so quickly.

About TREES...

It's all coming back
to me now ... whoops.

Tom

Imagine my surprise when I came
across this book on TREES ...
and realized I had read the back
somewhere before?

Your REVIEW HOMEWORK on trees,
Tom.

No more copying.

I want a new review done quickly
or another letter goes home to
your parents ... again.

Mr Fullerman

Point taken.

TREES:

This book aims to give you many interesting facts on trees. From where the largest tree in the world is, to how much food and shelter a tree can provide for wildlife.

Did you know that trees are the longest-living organisms on earth?

And that one acre of trees takes away nearly 2.6 tons of carbon dioxide each year?

The worlds oldest trees are thought to be 46,000-year-old BRISTLECONE pines that are in the USA. There are so many benefits that trees bring to our cities and many communities. They provide beauty and shade. Trees can make you feel serene and peaceful.

I hope the information in this book will inspire you to enjoy trees and plant more of them.

By A. Corn

BAD NEWS ⚡ ☆

Mr Fullerman has REMOVED one of my GOLD STARS ☆ from my chart until I hand in the new piece of review homework. **"LAST CHANCE, Tom,"** he tells me. I can see that Marcus has a LOT more gold stars than I do. Which is annoying.

Mr Fullerman even gave him a gold star for **"collecting an unusual beetle"**.

Which was REALLY irritating because I saw ⊙ ⊙ it first!

But he's WAY ahead of the whole class, even Amy. How's that happened?

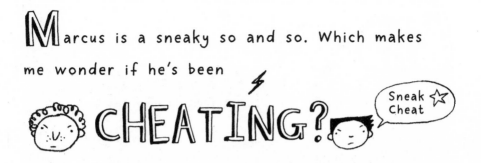

arcus is a sneaky so and so. Which makes
me wonder if he's been

CHEATING?

Sneak ☆
Cheat

n the way home, I am discussing my
suspicions about Marcus with Derek, who wants
to get some fruit chews from the shop.

And guess who's already there?

➡ 😠 ↙ **MARCUS.**

We say "Hi" but he's too
busy looking for something ...
and it's NOT sweets.

Suspicious ⬇

Gold star stickers

Derek picks out a few fruit chews 🟫 while I read this week's copy of **ROCK WEEKLY** (I'm off sweets due to my dodgy tooth 🦷 ... for now).

When we leave the shop I notice that MARCUS is standing in the section that has paper, envelopes ✉ and ... stickers.

"That's odd," I say to Derek as we leave the shop.

"I wonder what Marcus was buying?"

He's DEFINITELY up to something.

So we decide to take a peek through the shop window.

Sure enough...

There's Marcus buying what looks like a very

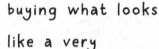 of GOLD STAR STICKERS ☆☆☆☆☆

I knew it! Marcus has been adding his own stars to the chart. Catching him out won't be easy, though. I will need VERY BEADY EYES like Mr Fullerman's. ⊙ ⊙

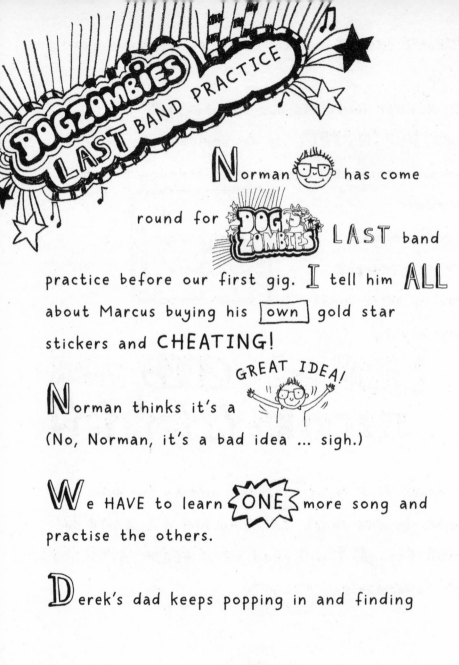

DOGZOMBIES LAST BAND PRACTICE

Norman has come round for **DOGZOMBIES** **LAST** band practice before our first gig. I tell him **ALL** about Marcus buying his own gold star stickers and **CHEATING!**

Norman thinks it's a GREAT IDEA!

(No, Norman, it's a bad idea ... sigh.)

We HAVE to learn ONE more song and practise the others.

Derek's dad keeps popping in and finding

excuses to come and see us rehearse.

Everything OK?

Even though we have ALL learnt

NOT to CHAT to Mr Fingle about music

(unless you have TEN HOURS ⊖ ⊖
to spare), right now we NEED his help.
Derek asks if he could suggest a good song for
us to learn ... today?

"Leave it to me, lads..."

(He's VERY excited.) He takes
out a Deep Purple record.

Another CLASSIC and perfect for you.

We work hard with Mr Fingle's help.

So **DOGZOMBIES** (that's us) have managed
to add

to our gig list.

RESULT!

Norman already knows how to play it and me
and Derek try our best. The singing is tricky,
especially when Mr Fingle keeps joining in.

Smoke on the water

Let's hope we've done enough to keep Granddad's teeth FIRMLY in his mouth on Sunday.

Now we've finished practising, Derek is looking for the last of the fruit chews he saved as a treat. But he can't find them anywhere. I haven't eaten them.

But I think I know who has...

It's a warning to us that

DOGZOMBIES FIRST-EVER GIG

YEAH!

BRILLIANT NEWS!

ED →

Delia's boyfriend has actually lent me

a REAL **ELECTRIC** guitar

and amp so I can play

REALLY **LOUDLY!**

From the look on Delia's face, it's all working fine.

Dad says he's coming along as our

"ROADIE" to help set everything up. He's taking it all very seriously

(and he's made a long list).

DOGZOMBIES
banner ✓
BAND ✓
INSTRUMENTS ✓
POSTERS ✓
EARPLUGS ✓
DRINKS ✓

Mum is busy with her camera.

While we have our first **BAND PHOTO** done,

Dad keeps doing
embarrassing rock-star poses.

Me and **D**erek are a bit **nervous**.
Norman is always so jumpy that you can't
tell if he is or not.

I have a lucky escape when Mum tries to
HUG me and wishes the band

good luck.

$\mathbb{D}$elia is her usual charming self.

You still here?

$\mathbb{D}$ad has packed the car and stuffed the roof rack. Then we're off to meet Granddad. It's only when we're driving that I realize...

We have NO idea where exactly we're playing our first gig.

$\mathbb{D}$ad says it will be a NICE $\mathbb{BIG}$

SURPRISE...

for us!

"LEAFY GREEN OLD
FOLKS' HOME ... ?" I say.

Granddad says they'll LOVE us.

"I have lots of friends here who are
looking 👁 👁 forward to seeing you!"

REALLY?
"And it won't matter how loud /// you play or
if you make any mistakes because MOST of the
audience are a bit hard of hearing. Just have
some fun!"

Great. I'm wondering just how much "fun"
the old folk are really going to have listening
to us?

Pardon?

Granddad has put up LOTS of posters around the home already. He's now telling everyone that I'm his grandson and that DOGZOMBIES are going to be

THE NEXT BIG THING.

So they must come and see us.

(Thanks, Granddad.)

We have to wait for the lounge to be FREE before we can set up.

And I manage to avoid a potential disaster by keeping Norman away from the tray of biscuits. PHEW!

STEP AWAY!

We've got quite a crowd now, but it takes a while for the old folk to get settled and comfy.

When Granddad introduces us, he says,

"Can you all hear me back there?"
Which sets off everyone saying
"Pardon?" "Eh?" "Pardon?"
Never mind, we can play loudly.
Then Granddad says, "Let's give
a WARM LEAFY GREEN welcome
to the amazing ... DOGZOMBIES."

And it's over to us to start with a rousing edition of "Delia's a Weirdo" (which seems to all go down well).

The sign on the door reads:

Tea and biscuits
(and band playing)
Today

Our first-ever gig was ... OK. Not brilliant ... just OK. (Room for improvement.) We made a few mistakes, but no one seemed to notice.

All in all, we had a good time, Norman didn't go too wild and Granddad's teeth stayed firmly in place the whole time, which is a good sign, I think? And I heard a few people singing

"Delia's a WEIRDO" when we left.

Result! ☺

 Granddad says there are a lot of other old folks' homes we could play. "Everyone has to start somewhere!" he reminds us.

       True.

(I wonder where **DUDE3** played their first gig?)

Back at home I'm reading

Delia's copy of **ROCK WEEKLY**

and imagining that

DOGZOMBIES are being

interviewed by the magazine about the success
of their first-ever gig (and other important
music matters).

OLDIES ROCK OUT TO DOGZOMBIES' FIRST GIG!

Rock Weekly: So, Tom, who are your INFLUENCES for DOGZOMBIES?

Tom: That's a very good question. All sorts of things, really. DUDE3 are a huge influence. And I'm often inspired to write songs by VERY irritating family members.

RW: "Delia's a Weirdo"?

Tom: I couldn't have said it better myself...

RW: Why did you play your first gig at an old folks' home? It's an interesting choice.

Tom: Old folk like good music too. What can I say, we have a growing grey fan base who are spreading the DOGZOMBIE word!

RW: What's in the future for DOGZOMBIES?

Tom: World domination, I think, and a sponsorship deal with a delicious biscuit company would be nice?

Delia rudely interrupts me.

Are you pretending to be interviewed?

"No," I say unconvincingly.

You are! SADDO. ha! ha!

Then she takes back her copy of
ROCK WEEKLY and goes off
LAUGHING!

Ha! Ha! Ha! Ha!

I think the next song I write will be called "My Sister is an **IDIOT**". I have lots of ideas already.

Fresh from our **SUCCESSFUL** first-ever gig, me, Derek and Norman are reliving the **WHOLE** event in school.

I say, "There were **loads** of people all cheering and clapping."

Which is *SORT* of true. ☺

I don't mention it was at the LEAFY GREEN OLD FOLKS' HOME either.

In class, everyone is settling down when Mrs Mumble makes an announcement over the tannoy.

WILL TOM Gates and Norman Watson and Derek Fingle come to the School office TO See MR KEEN ...

Mr Fullerman is looking at me with his "what have you been up to now?" stare as we leave.

Derek is already waiting outside the school office.

"What do you think Mr Keen wants?" he asks me.

"Who knows ... whatever it is, we're innocent," I say.

Norman's just happy to be out of lessons.

YEAH!

Turns out that Mr Keen has had a phone call from the owner of the LEAFY GREEN OLD FOLKS' HOME

saying how impressed they were with the band. Apparently we're

"a credit to the school".

"Well done, all three of you,"

 Mr Keen says.

Then he goes and SP☺ILs

EVERYTHING by telling us,

"You'll be even better in the school band now!"

Mr Sprocket is running a special school band practice this lunchtime.

"I'll be showing some new parents around the school. It will be VERY impressive for them to see the band in action. Isn't that a good idea?"

(Eeeeeerrrrr, NO!)

NOT the school band again.

Mr Keen is DETERMINED to put us in the school band!

WHY? Looking at Derek I can see he's not wild about the idea.
(Especially after last time.)

Norman doesn't seem to care because he's just spotted a spider walking up the wall.

I'm trying to think of YET another excuse to get OUT of this situation.
(Think! Mmmm ... mmmmm... Think! Mmmmmm...)
All kinds of ideas are going through my head.

Then it comes to me in a

F L A S H!

"**Mr Keen**," I say.

"Yes, Tom."

"Would you mind if we DIDN'T play in the school band? We were SO RUBBISH at playing the recycled instruments last time. It was terrible. Everyone thought so."

   "Oh ... are you all sure?"
Mr Keen asks.

"Very," I say.
Derek and Norman are nodding too.

PHEW! Look of relief

WHY didn't I think of saying that before?
And just like that, it's all sorted.
No more school band.

WRONG!

INSTEAD...

M r Keen says that **DOG ZOMBIES** 🎵🎵 can play a special gig

in front of the

WHOLE ENTIRE

SCHOOL.

"Just like you did for the
LEAFY GREEN OLD FOLKS' HOME.

So well done Tom for suggesting that," he adds.

(I didn't ... groan.)

On the way back to class I tell Derek and Norman it will all be fine because Mr Keen will probably forget about it. (He won't.)

"We're not ready to play in front of the school yet," I say.

We all agree on that.

ack in class.

I'm hoping Mr Fullerman might have heard the
news that Mr Keen was VERY pleased with
us (for a change). I might even get a bit of
PRAISE?
No, nothing yet. Oh well.

I get ready to join in the "class reading",
which is a nice and easy lesson.

I've even remembered to sneak a copy of

ROCK WEEKLY into my reading
book just in case things gets a bit dull.
(Emergency reading, I call it.)
    But Mr Fullerman says I'm EXCUSED from
class reading today because I still haven't given
in my REVIEW HOMEWORK.

"Have you, TOM?"

And if I don't finish it **NOW** I will have to do it at lunch time in the library, with Miss Page keeping an eye on me.

"You don't want ANOTHER letter home, do you, Tom?"

"No, Mr Fullerman."

"And no copying books on trees."

Groan.

Marcus is sniggering next to me. He says, "No gold stars for cheating", which is irritating.

OK. I'll do a REVIEW of **DOGZOMBIES'** first gig. It's fresh in my memory and shouldn't take long. I'll get it done before lunch.

I don't want to be stuck in the library, after all.

In the library
I'm still finishing off
my homework.

I can hear people laughing and
PLAYING outside and the school band practising
in the hall. Miss Page → is keeping
an EYE 👁 on me and a couple of
other kids too.

(At least I'm not in the school band any more
... that's something.)

I'm hoping this review homework will be worth

SIX MERITS and 3 gold stars

Because right now Marcus is STILL in the lead on the CHART. Although I'm convinced he's been

CHEATING, Cheat?

I can't prove it, which is annoying.

So I'm trying to get the last bit of my homework finished when I glance up and stare out of the window. I notice something a bit ODD.

From where I'm sitting in the library, I can see RIGHT INTO our CLASSROOM. SOMEONE is in there.

It doesn't look like Mr Fullerman, Mr Keen or any of the teachers.

I can't see who it is. So I keep watching.

I STAND UP

for a closer look.

Just when they duck down

under the desks.

Which is **VERY** suspicious.

The school band are still playing, so it can't be any of them (or Mr Sprocket).

Whoever it is has curly hair. I can see the top of their head moving closer

and closer

and closer

towards

THE GOLD STAR AWARD CHART

I knew it!

This could be my chance to catch

a very sneaky

CHEAT.

Smug

I ask Miss Page if I can leave.

←Classroom · All done

"Because Mr Fullerman
wants to check my
FINISHED REVIEW

HOMEWORK himself."
(Good thinking.)

Then I do super *FAST*
walking to get to the classroom.
   I'm SO nearly there when I
BUMP
right into Mr Keen.
Who is busy showing
the new parents
around the school.

He asks me what I'm doing in school at lunch
time?
I say EXTRA studying
        (which is sort of true).

(318)

Then Mr Keen tells the parents ALL about **DOGZOMBIES**

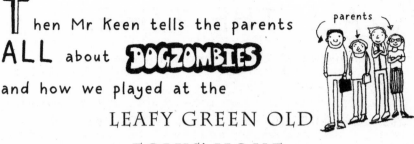
parents

and how we played at the

LEAFY GREEN OLD FOLKS' HOME.

(He's going on a bit. Blah ... blah blah...)

I'm DESPERATE to get to the classroom!

Then just when I think he's finished chatting...

hello

Mr Fullerman turns up!

And |HE| starts talking to the parents about **"the school field trip"** and what kind of work we do in class.

BLAH BLAH BLAH!

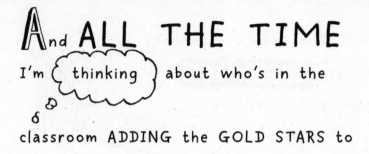

And **ALL THE TIME**

I'm (thinking) about who's in the

classroom ADDING the GOLD STARS to

the **CHART** !

When one of the **PARENTS** asks me,

What do YOU like about your school, Tom?

And **THAT'S**

when I get one of my TOTAL

BRAIN WAVES

I say...

"I really like the

GOLD STAR AWARD CHART

because it encourages you to do well

in class."

(Superb answer.)

"Sounds interesting," they say.

"How does it work?"

 Mr Keen suggests I

might like to show them in my

classroom.

And I say, "That's an EXCELLENT ☺

idea, follow me."

Walking to the classroom I explain to the parents how we **EARN** merits for good work. And **TWO MERITS** equals

And the **ONLY** person who is allowed

to give out the gold stars is

MR FULLERMAN.

"You are **DEFINITELY NOT** allowed

to stick the stars on yourself,

 are you,

Mr Fullerman?"

I say.

"No, Tom, that's my job. And I hand out prizes at the end of term to whoever has the most gold stars."

We're nearly outside the classroom now.

So I say,

"If Mr Fullerman EVER caught someone adding their OWN stars to the chart, that would be cheating, wouldn't it, Mr Fullerman?"

"Yes, Tom, it would be," he says.

Then I OPEN the classroom door, and just as I suspected...

There's Marcus Meldrew with a whole packet of his own gold stars.

(He's busted.)

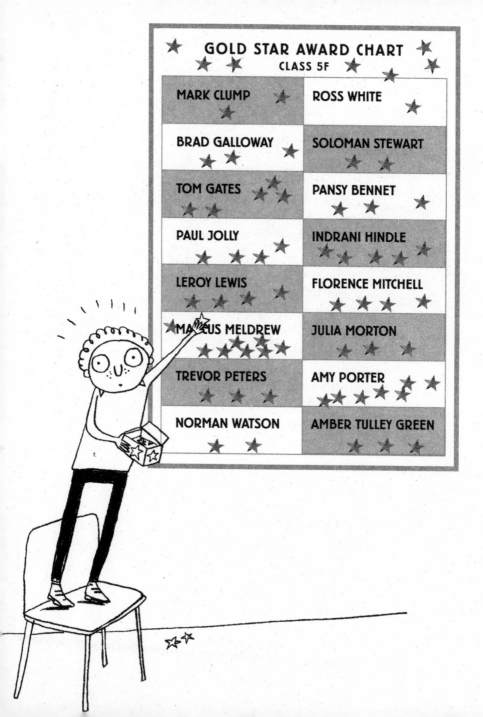

Dear Mr and Mrs Meldrew

I am very disappointed to tell you that Marcus has been caught adding his own stars to the GOLD STAR AWARD CHART. In other words, he's been caught cheating.

Marcus will be missing playtimes for the next three days and helping Miss Page in the library as a punishment.

Along with writing an apology letter to me.

I hope Marcus has learnt his lesson, as he is capable of earning his own stars without cheating.

Kind regards

Mr Fullerman

Class 5F Form Tutor

Due to Marcus CHEATING ...

his stars have been removed.

So now I'm (only) TWO STARS AWAY

from AMY PORTER (who's in the lead).

I need to get four merits (or more) for my
REVIEW HOMEWORK on the
DOGZOMBIES gig.

Mr Fullerman has been taking **AGES**
to mark my work.
When he does give it back to me he says
there's been a bit of a problem.

WHAT NOW?

Sorry, Tom.

I had a bit of an accident with my coffee!

Luckily it missed your homework and I was able to read and mark it finally.

Please make sure you do homework on time in future?

Mr Fullerman

FIRST-EVER GIG

REVIEW HOMEWORK AGAIN.

(For the ~~SECOND~~ THIRD TIME)

By Tom Gates.

If I was the lead singer of **DUDE 3** I might be a tiny bit disappointed finding out the venue for the gig was THE LEAFY GREEN OLD FOLKS' HOME. But for **DOGZOMBIES'** first gig it was excellent.

My granddad BOB arranged it all (thanks, Granddad).

We had to carry a LOT of stuff into the home to set up.

(330)

Well ... when I say "WE", I mean my dad, who was our roadie for the day.

Before we could get started we had to wait for the

USE
IT OR
LOSE
IT
YOGA
CLASS

to finish.

Then **D**ad wasn't allowed to use the **BIG** hammer he brought to put up our

STOP!

DOGZOMBIES

banner.

Luckily the surgical tape worked just as well.

SURGICAL TAPE

Granddad said,

"Everyone who lives here is coming to see you because they are all

But I'm not so sure that's true. Because outside there was a sign that said tea and biscuits and band playing.

I managed to **STOP** Norman from eating any biscuits before the gig started in case he went

(again).

It took a LONG time for everyone to get seated and comfortable.

And even l o n g e r for us to start playing.

This was mostly because:

1. I completely forgot what song we were starting with. And we had to start again twice.

2. Norman accidentally knocked over a cymbal, which made a

MAssivE CRASH.

3. **S**ome of the OLD FOLK got a BIT of a

SHOCK from the noise

and needed a top-up of tea and a biscuit

to calm down.

That's better.

4. **V**era in the second row couldn't see

Vera

 properly because **Alfie's** head

was in the way. So Dad had

to help Vera to a better seat.

5. **F**inally ... we were just about to get

started when FRED wanted to

know why we were called

DOGZOMBIES .

Which was a good question and took a bit of explaining.

EVENTUALLY ... we did start playing. "Delia's a WEIRDO" went down well. So did " ".

But the best song of all was "SMOKE ON THE WATER".

Because everyone joined in by tapping the sides of their teacups in time with the music.

Tap

The whole GIG went SO well that at the end we got a
STANDING OVATION...

Which is not easy to do

when the most of the audience

is well over

The End

Six merits, Tom, and
THREE GOLD STARS.

WELL DONE!

Mr Fullerman

HOORAY!

Oh yes ... see those extra stars twinkling on the award chart!

Excellent!

GOLD STAR AWARD CHART
CLASS 5F

MARK CLUMP	ROSS WHITE
BRAD GALLOWAY	SOLOMAN STEWART
TOM GATES	PANSY BENNET
PAUL JOLLY	INDRANI HINDLE
LEROY LEWIS	FLORENCE MITCHELL
MARCUS MELDREW	JULIA MORTON
TREVOR PETERS	AMY PORTER
NORMAN WATSON	AMBER TULLEY GREEN

Question

What has Spots
Not many gold 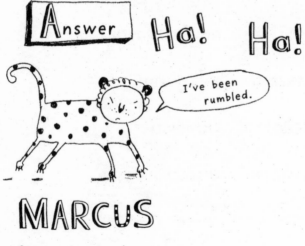stars
(NOW)

And looks slightly less smug than usual

Answer   Ha!   Ha!

I've been
rumbled.

MARCUS
(the cheater)

Finished reading
this book ALREADY?
You might like the same kind

of FUNNY stuff I do.
So check out my BLOG

tomgatesworld.blogspot.com

More doodles.
More DOGZOMBIES
and sadly more Marcus.

Why don't you check out my new

Every

Amc

Long

iary...

hings

zing (sort of)

dog

All my own work

Published by
Scholastic 2011

Good stuff

toom

I won a MASSIVE
pack of pens for coming (nearly)
TOP of the Gold Star Chart
AND a huge bar of chocolate
(eaten).

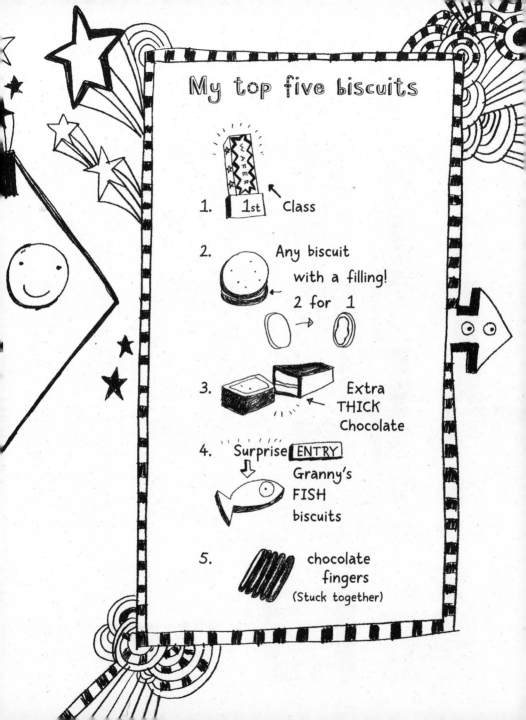

My top five biscuits

1. 1st Class

2. Any biscuit with a filling! 2 for 1

3. Extra THICK Chocolate

4. Surprise ENTRY Granny's FISH biscuits

5. chocolate fingers (Stuck together)

Have You Got ALL the TOM GATES books yet?